The Murderer's Apprentice

To Curtiss

All the best

Rory.

R.W. HEGARTY

©Copyright by R.W. Hegarty 2008.

First Edition

The author asserts the moral right under the
Copyright, Designs and Patents Act 1988 to be
identified as the author of this work.

All rights reserved. No part of this publication may
be reproduced, stored in a retrieval system, or
transmitted, in any form or by any means without the
prior written consent of the author, nor be otherwise
circulated in any form of binding or cover other than
that in which it is published and without a similar
condition being imposed on the subsequent
purchaser.

Published by YouWriteOn.com

ABOUT THE AUTHOR

R.W. Hegarty was born in Halifax in 1966.
He now lives in Mortlake, west London with
his wife and young daughter. He has worked
as a journalist and press officer, but
suspicion persists that he prefers idling
about doing nothing. *The Murderer's
Apprentice* is his first novel.

To Jo and Cara

1. A Life Less Ordinary

Murderers are born, not made.

That's what Keith said the day he took me on, that's what my Dad always said when recalling famous serial killers from the days before the Enterprise Act.

It's a bit like being a footballer or a pop star – many are called, but few are chosen. Let's be honest, we've all thought about murdering somebody at some point in our lives. The cheating spouse, the noisy neighbour, the bitter rival, the irritating **boss**...but how many of us go through with it? Only a tiny minority – those with the drive, the skill – the *madness*, I suppose. That's what Keith always said. The greatest murderers are all mad.

For me, murder wasn't so much a career move as one of those things I drifted into. I'd done my GCSEs, my A levels, my degree in Business Studies. It was a question of where to go next. A part time job in a bar while I considered my options? Travel the world on a shoestring? Or take up killing? If I wanted to be less ordinary – and I *desperately* did - there was only one option.

The problem was, I'd always been average, at everything. I performed averagely well enough at school to go to an average university and get an average degree. I looked like everyone else – average height, average build, average shoe size. I used to think I was walking around with a label on me that said "ordinary" - except that in itself would have been exceptional. However much I tried to stand out, I just blended in. More than anything, all my life, I'd wanted be less fucking *ordinary*.

I was also at a low ebb. I'd just been dumped by Miranda, my fat, ginger ex-girlfriend, who had realised that I didn't fancy her, any more than she fancied me. Two years we'd been humping away at one other, whilst closing our eyes and picturing someone else. You can get away with that for a surprisingly long time. Mutual discovery is as rare as mutual climax, but on the day when she shouted "Ohhhh, Billy!" at the same moment as I murmured Rosie's name, all hell broke loose.

It seemed unfair that it broke loose exclusively in my direction. I know Miranda had always (rightly) suspected I had a crush on Rosie and now her worst fears had been confirmed. I know that when girlfriends are angry, it is generally hard to get a word in sideways. But I felt she got away with the Billy thing far too easily. I mean, the only Billy she knew was her *brother*.

It is also difficult to defend yourself whilst removing a condom after an extensive, illicit-fantasy-fuelled orgasm. Miranda, having housed but not personally inspired said orgasm, was livid. "That fucking cocky little silly little big titted *bitch*! I *knew* you fancied her! You *wanker*!"

There was no disputing any of it, especially not the big titted bit, nor indeed the wanker. I was backing away as I pulled off the condom, trying to say something about Billy, which mysteriously came out as "I can't help it, I love her!" Miranda punched me then, hard in the face, a good punch, and I got my lower body up off the bed quickly, out of the reach of her feet.

"You *love* her?! Just fuck right off! You just want to shag her and you can't, so you shagged me instead! For two years! You *wanker!*" As she bellowed the 'w' word again, she threw one of my shoes across the room, smashing her bedroom mirror.

"You can pay for that as well!"

I stood in silence, looking at the naked fat ginger girl who I had almost certainly just had hot, grungy sex with for the final time. She glared back. I opened my mouth to speak.

My other shoe flew ferociously into the silence.

"Sean, fuck *off* out of my life. And don't *ever* come back!"

I closed my mouth again, picked up my shoes and my clothes and stumbled out of her life.

And that was the day I started to take it all seriously. This mad dream of being a murderer. It began with me thinking that there must be more to life than this and ended with me vowing to myself that I was going to do something very special, something ultra- glamorous, after university. No poncing off to some faceless company full of faceless blenders-in. I was going to do something so big, so exciting, that nobody would ever scream their brother's name when they having sex with me again. I was going to be *extraordinary*.

2. The Cheat

Cheating always had a tinge of glamour when you saw it in films and soaps, Rosie reflected as Shirley snored beside her. But in real life - in everyday, humdrum, run-of-the-mill lives - it felt a bit sordid and a lot inconvenient.

It wasn't just the logistics, which were difficult enough in themselves – you can't be in two places at one time if it's one person's birthday and another just got a new job. No, it was conversations that were the worst – remembering which stories you'd told which lover, which alibis you'd given them and, as time went on, which lies you'd told other people to preserve your double life.

The evasion bit – the being seen somewhere you shouldn't – filled her with a sense of dull panic rather than excitement, and had for as long as she could remember. But unless she was literally caught with her pants down or at least mid-snog, she could usually get away with it. If someone thinks you're a lesbian, they will think nothing of seeing you with a man. And if they think you're straight, they will think any woman they see you with is a different type of girlfriend. The challenge was to keep the two worlds apart, as each began to grow to the point where they almost touched at the edges.

Shirley and Rosie had been lovers for five years. Since before Uni, before London. It had all started very innocently, with a Big Crush on her friend. She had found herself secretly thrilled by some of Shirley's accounts of her sexual experiences with boys, she herself having had comparatively few.

She'd looked up to Shirley, who seemed more confident, more together.

Growing up, Rosie had increasingly found that she fancied girls as well as boys. She knew this was No Big Deal, but it was also something she had never shared with anyone. Shirley had a body that a 17 year old girl mistakenly thinks is to die for: tall and slim with long legs, no real curves, no flab. She had mousy blonde hair, clear grey eyes and blemish-free skin. All carried with a swagger and certainty that Rosie had never felt. Sometimes, Shirley and her stories and her seemed to fill her mind all day and then creep into her dreams at night.

Then there had been the last day before she went off to Uni in Manchester, when a group of them had gone out together and got trashed. Rosie couldn't quite remember how it had happened. She had ended up drinking vodka in Shirley's Mum's lounge, and woken up in Shirley's bed, naked and entwined with her friend. She still had no memory of the previous evening, but when Shirley had rolled over and kissed her, it had felt right. In fact, it had felt like the most right, amazing, exciting thing that had ever happened to her. She'd kissed Shirley back with interest and so began a passionate, intimate and almost entirely secret love affair.

It hadn't been all sweetness and light. She'd felt weird when Shirley confessed years later that she'd never had sex with anyone else, that her stories were all fantasies she had made up to impress Rosie. "I've fancied you since we were 14," Shirley had laughed. "I always knew I was a lezza!"

10

This made Rosie uncomfortable. She'd confided in the past to Shirley how she'd felt about various boys and she didn't think she could take it all back now and say she'd been lying as well – though she did feel Shirley half expected her to. But what freaked her out even more was the fact that their whole story had changed overnight. Whatever way you looked at it, her initial Big Crush on Shirley had been built on her friend's lies and deceptions. Suddenly, Shirley was not and never had been the self-assured, promiscuous flirt she had fallen in love with. That was a very strange thing to come to terms with.

It was not a good time. She was stressed out working towards her final exams and Shirley was giving her a hard time about all the secrecy surrounding their relationship – Rosie hadn't told her mates in Manchester, let alone her family. As far as the people in her student life were concerned, Shirley was just an old schoolmate who occasionally came to visit. Shirley – who had fewer friends to confide in and rarely spoke to her parents – was starting to feel like a dirty secret.

"Why does no-one know about us?" she would whine. "Why can't we behave like a normal couple?"

Rosie didn't know the answer – except she didn't feel that they *were* a normal couple. She was still attracted to other people and occasionally acting on that attraction. Shirley's clinginess was a big turn-off.

Inevitably, it was at this time that she'd met Ben, who was a student at her University. Ben was chilled out, funny, everything that Shirley was not. And he had these deep, dark brown eyes that you could just get lost in.

Many times, in the one and a half years since she'd been seeing Ben, she had thought of ending it with one or both of them. But Shirley was just too big a part of her life to imagine it without her, and her new romance with Ben was too much fun to let go – even when he'd started getting a bit clingy as well. And when she'd graduated and got the job in the PR department for British American Heroin, she and Shirley had moved to London – and living a double life between London and Manchester was much easier than between Manchester and Stoke. London was so much bigger and easier to hide in.

The doorbell interrupted her thoughts and she untangled herself from Shirley's embrace and went to answer it. There was always that nagging fear that one day she would do that and it would be Ben having tracked her down. He still didn't have her London address, just her number, and this was a growing source of tension. Plus the fact that she'd cancelled him last night and he was angry about it, as it was his birthday. But what could she do – Rosie had just got a new job and had dragged her out to celebrate.

She opened the door. Thank fuck. It was Sean, the Boy Next Door.

"Hi," she smiled.

"Hi," he smiled back.

They stood in silence, Rosie slightly self-conscious in her dressing gown.

"Er – I'm at a – loose end. Could I take your cat for a walk?"

Rosie stared at him.

"Cats don't do walkies, dickhead!" came a muffled voice from inside. Rosie smiled apologetically.

Sean stood there smiling back, until a naked Shirley appeared, pushed Rosie out of the way and slammed the door in his face.

3. The Mass Murderer

This was a scary moment.

Keith Hartley was built like the proverbial brick shithouse. About 6'4 in height, with thinning grey hair, broad shoulders and upper arms which seemed thicker than my entire frame.

His shop consisted of very little – just a desk, a couple of filing cabinets and a large framed picture of him, some old newspaper cutting. It had once been a kebab shop and Keith had never quite got rid of the smell of grease and fat. I walked in the front door, which opened inwards, and there was a counter to my right – meaning Keith Hartley was effectively behind the door. The counter had on it a phone and some of Keith's cards, nothing else. The floor was bare and the climate cold.

He stood facing me across his desk, arms bulging, T-shirt rippling. Eyes glaring defiantly. And I hadn't even said hello yet.

"Yep?" he barked.

My throat had gone dry. Was this his interviewing technique?

"Er – I'm looking for a job."

He tried to smile, but his face was too hard to perform the contortions. It came over as a malevolent glare.

"Bisniss?" he barked back.

"No! No, not ... business. I mean – I'm looking for a job. For work."

He smirked – he was getting nearer to that smiling thing – and said nothing.

When there's a silence, it seems to be etiquette for the more nervy person present to fill it. And I was feeling distinctly nervy.

"Do you – are you – looking for someone?"

Keith snorted. "I've no need of a tea boy if that's what ya mean."

"Ahaha!" I gulped. "I was thinking more of – an assistant. A helper. Do you take on – er – trainees in your line of business?"

He did it. He smiled. Jackpot.

Then he laughed uproariously.

"Tray-knees! What the fook college 'ave you just crawled outta? Tray-knees! Fook's sake!" He shook with laughter.

I was shaking as well. "Er – just looking for a chance. To prove myself?"

He folded his arms, still just managing to smile, ferociously.

"Tell me, Lad. Has tha ever killed owt?"

"N-no. Er – flies, maybe?"

"Flies, eh? And what's my line o' trade?"

"You're – ah. Well, you're a - murderer."

In a brisk movement, he was out from behind the desk. And his hand was on my shoulder, guiding me towards the door.

"Check this out, Lad," he said gruffly, pushing me though the door and forcing my neck back – for a terrified second, I thought he was going to snap it. I found myself looking at the sign outside his shop.

KEITH HARTLEY
MASS MURDERER

"Now, what does that say?"

"M-mass murderer?"

"That's reight. Not mur-derer! *Mass* murderer!" He clapped me on the back and led me back into the shop.

"An' worra bout this?" Still holding me by the back of the neck, he led me in behind the desk, to where his enlarged, framed news cutting almost filled the wall.

SERIAL KILLER HARTLEY GETS LIFE, read the headline.

"Y-you were in prison?"

"Too right. Before t'Enterprise Act, killin' folk were a crime. You won't remember that. An' I were at it then. Killed five or six of 'em up in Wigan before I got copped."

"So – they let you out again then?"

He snorted indignantly. "Well course they did! Dark ages were over! You can't keep a bloke in 't'slammer when yuv made 'is bisniss legal! All I'm sayin' is – I were in this game before. For fun! Long before them Johnny-cum-lately tossers wi' their girly guns and their fancy explosions! I've killed more people than you've 'ad 'ot dinners – an' I tell ya – mur-derers are born, not made."

He finally released his grip.

"But I'm keen," I squeaked. "I could learn. I could help you!"

He laughed again, emphasising the creases on his huge brow.

"What's yer name, Son?"

"Sean."

"Well, Shawn, I like yer style. Fair play to ya. Comin' in ere lookin' for a job! But I don't need some soft student type gerrin' in ma way. I make good money. Easy money. Take you on? Well, there's nowt in it for me!"

I tried again. "What will happen to your business? After you die?"

"Fook all. I won't care."

"But I could keep it going…keep the name alive?"

"I really won't give a fook. I'll be six feet under an' glad of it."

I tried again. "But have you never wanted to – pass on your skills?"

"No can do. Like I say, mur-derers are born, not made."

He folded his arms. That seemed to be his last word on the subject.

"Ok. Nice meeting you anyway."

I shuffled off.

I don't really know what made Keith change his mind. He seemed determined he didn't want to take anyone on and his reasons were pretty clear. Nor did he seem the type to change his view. Maybe his own explanation is as good as any - as he said to me later: "Maybe I thought you 'ad it. The madness."

But as I put my hand on the door that day, he called me back. And many, many times since, I've wished he hadn't.

4. The Bleeding Heart

Betsy Saunders hummed silently to herself and not just because she had her Earpod in. The sound of Oasis 3, she thought, was very much like Oasis 2, which had been pretty much a note-for-note copy of the original Oasis from fifty odd years ago. It was very impressive and entirely expected. But Oasis 3 alone would not drown out the boring twat that was Richard Splash, who was facing her across the Kellogs House of Commons chamber.

Splash had recently been appointed to the Cabinet as the new Minister for Free Enterprise. A skinny, high-pitched young man, with greasy, side-parted hair, vile skin and yellow teeth, Splash had a swagger that did not match his appearance. He had been droning on for half an hour or so about new legislation to increase the competitiveness of Police UK.

His concern was that new kids on the block, like CrimeBusters Inc., were taking all the business away from Police UK, the former state-run monopoly. The problem, Splash insisted, was red tape. While nearly forty years of Coalition Party Government - and especially the Enterprise Act of 2030 - had done a great deal to end restrictive practices, some still remained. And one was the fact that companies like Police UK were not allowed to charge customers more than £10 per investigation. CrimeBusters Inc, who were not in existence when the Enterprise Act came in, were not restricted in this way.

"It is now twenty years," droned Splash, "Since the gweatest Chancellor this countwy has ever had, Sir Camewon Blair, intwoduced the Enterpwise Act. At the time, he put in the eminently sensible pwecaution that the newly-pwivatised police force would not charge people on lower incomes for investigations. Ten years later, we intwoduced a maximum charge of £10.

"It is now ten years since that change, and time to wevisit the scenawio. Police UK is disadvantaged in an ever-gwowing market – and fwankly, this is the most open economy in the world. If people do not have the wherewithal to pay the going wate for a police inquiry, then fwankly that is a wesult of their own fecklessness."

He'd paused to grin, showing his yellow teeth and enjoying the chortles of his colleagues, and it was at that point that Betsy had started listening to Oasis 3.

What on earth kind of world did we live in? It was already virtually impossible to get Police UK to investigate anything. Only last week, two of her Islington North constituents had complained of an unlicensed burglary at their premises. It was quite clear that the perpetrators had been amateurs, by the very fact that they'd smashed a window, broken crockery, left prints everywhere and taken only the least valuable items. Mr and Mrs Green were understandably enraged: the insurance company would laugh it off as an inside job and refuse to pay out. This freelance burglary was on the increase, people without training, operating without licences – but Police UK were refusing to take the case on.

Betsy had been a People's Party MP for six years, all of them in opposition, often to her own party as well as the Government. She had a reputation as something of a firebrand, an extremist. This was because she thought it was time to look again at legislation like the Enterprise Act. More protection, not less, was what her constituents needed. But this was not a view shared by Richard Splash – or indeed her own Party's leadership.

The People's Party had been formed in 2020, a few months after the Great Coalition, when the three main parties in British politics had come to the realisation that they basically agreed on pretty much everything and should unite in a single party. They had actually agreed this in 2018, but had then spent two years wrangling about the name, which was the only remaining point they disagreed on. Should they be the Labour Conservative Democrats, The Conservative Labour Liberals, New Labour, New Conservatives, New Liberals…the arguments seemed to go on forever. Eventually, they settled for being the Coalition Party.

Newspaper columnists declared the end of politics, the Socialist Workers Party called for a general strike and the founders of the People's Party set about doing something to prevent the Coalition Party forming a permanent government. The People's Party was basically formed from the small rump of those in the Labour and Lib Dem parties who didn't agree with the Great Coalition, Green parties who accused the Coalition Party of doing nothing about the severe floods battering the country with increasing frequency, a few general do-gooders who thought there should be an opposition of some kind and a few old Conservatives and far left activists who thought the new party was something it wasn't. Over the years, the People's Party had moved so far from its founding principles of economic intervention, tackling climate change, redistributing wealth and maintaining a welfare state, that it had become unrecognisable. Now it just believed in 'people power'. Betsy wasn't quite sure what that meant, but she had a feeling that was the whole point.

She hadn't been listening to whatever Splash was twittering on about, but decided to intervene anyway and rose to her feet.

"DOES THE RIGHT HONOURABLE GENTLEMAN REALISE…?" she bellowed, then apologised and removed her earpod. The Coalition benches collapsed in laughter – as did many on her own side. She sat down again.

Splash savoured his moment. "Well, I suppose it was wather a long speech, but it is customawy on this side of the House to listen to a speaker before intervening in their speech. Perhaps the Honouwable Member's failure to listen reflects why she is so out of touch – even with members of her own Party!"

Betsy reddened, but rose again to her feet.

"I do apologise to the Right Honourable Gentleman. His speech was absolutely riveting. But does he realise…?"

Shit. Her mind had gone completely blank.

"Does he realise…?"

"Realise what?" crowed the benches opposite, in fits of giggles.

"Does he realise that …?"

It was no good. Just say *something*…

"…realise that the – the Enterprise Act - is a load of *crap*?"

Now both sides of the House collapsed again. Splash wiped imaginary tears of mirth from his eyes. On the front bench, Gregory Styles, Leader of the Opposition, swivelled around to glare at the Member for Islington North.

"What an informed, weasonable comment!" jousted Splash. "What wepartee! What perception! We have more people in employment than ever before! Lower cwime figures than ever before! More successful businesses than any other countwy in the world! All down to the histowic legislation she dismisses in such – *articulate* - terms!

"Perhaps the Leader of the Opposition agwees with the Honouwable Lady? Or at the vewy least, he must wealise that the pwesence of such extwemist views, such *bleeding hearts*, on the People's Party benches is the weason we Coalitionists will soon be celebwating thirty years in power!""

Betsy bowed her head. She was not having a good day. Outwitted by one of the biggest clods in the House. Splash's yellow teeth were gleaming in triumph. Gregory Styles was furious. And Oasis 3 were no better than Oasis 2.

5. Sleeping With Rosie

I met Rosie in the Hard Drug Cafe club, in Manchester. In the gents toilet, to be precise. She was plastered, incoherent and staggering. She stumbled in, took a swaying glance at the busy urinals, put her hand to her mouth in confusion and fell against the condom machine.

"Weyhey!" was the general consensus, but I was in Good Samaritan mode and went over to help her up. And don't you give me any crap about trying to get into her pants. She really wasn't looking very fanciable, with wet hair, streaked mascara and torn tights. I helped her to her feet and she looked at me dazed.

"You okay?"

Why do we *say* that? We see someone fall over, someone crying, someone flattened by a bulldozer, what's our first reaction? It's not 'can I help?' or 'do you need an ambulance?' or even 'quit snivelling, for God's sake'. It's 'Are you okay?'. Even though the answer is patently negative. And if they play along with the whole facade and say yes, they are okay, we refuse to believe them. 'Are you sure?' is the next prompt, then 'You don't look it'. That'll help. Bombard them with rhetorical questions, then tell them they look like a pile of shit.

Anyway, Rosie didn't seem to mind. She stumbled a little and held on to my arm, then gazed drunkenly into my eyes. "Hello."

The urinal crew were enjoying themselves, pissing on one another while turning around to watch.

"Talk about taking advantage, mate!" said one, to a chorus of laughter.

I tried gamely to smile off the insults while steadying her, which wasn't easy, as she slipped in a load of water and her legs went up in the air.

The urinal boys pissed themselves in more ways than one. I steered her out of the door, her still smiling at me in a care in the community kind of way.

"ARE YOU OKAY?" I shouted above the din.

Rosie looked at me, smiled, and tried to kiss me.

I pushed her back, holding her at arms' length. She stared at me.

"SORRY - ARE YOU OKAY?"

She nodded this time and I let go. Fatal error. She slid to the floor.

I bent down to try to pick her up again, and was joined by a member of the security staff. "Take your girlfriend home," he said, as he helped her to her feet, "She's wasted!"

I was going to go and look for Miranda and the others I was with, I truly was. But he was having none of it and more or less bodily removed us both, in spite of my protestations.

A weird silence hits you when you've been ejected from a club. When you leave at the same time as everyone else, there's plenty of people around to replicate the noise inside. But when you leave early, all is vast and silent, your ears ring and you suddenly feel like you've woken from a dream. This dream I had woken from with a drunk girl on my arm. I looked at her properly for the first time.

All those bits about streaky mascara and torn tights are true, but on the plus side, Rosie was absolutely gorgeous. She had these dark eyes that just asked you to accept her, love her. She was only small, which maybe added to the little girl lost appeal. As did the softest, most kissable mouth in England, curly scrunched up brown hair and the cool pink denim jacket she was wearing. And - as Miranda has already informed you - great tits. What a solid citizen I had been not to snog her back in the club!

"Right, let's get you a taxi," I said, in my taking-control-of-the-situation voice. "Where do you live?"

She looked back at me, still dazed. Then she burst into tears.

Rosie and I slept together that night. Not in the way you're thinking. Not in the way *I* started thinking from that point on. No, it was all very chaste. We went for a curry, which she couldn't eat, she told me her troubles and we shared a cab home. It turned out she was a Manchester Uni student too and lived just up the road from me.

She invited me in for coffee, which just meant coffee, and wasn't even coffee, as she decided to go straight to bed. Because the sofa was already occupied by a quilt and some groping student couple, she invited me up to her room and then fell asleep. I was about to leave, when she rolled over, stretched and patted the bed next to her.

"Sleep here tonight, Sean," she said.

Which just meant sleep.

And sleep wasn't far away. It's lucky I'd been doused in booze, as my young mind was whirling with what she'd just told me. Her trouble. It wasn't boyfriend trouble, but *girlfriend* trouble. And I don't mean a row with her mate. She was having a hard time with her lover, *Shirley!* The sexiest girl I had met all term was a *lesbian*! This was the stuff of fantasy.

Rosie's problem, as I understood it, was that she'd left Shirley at home in Stoke and Shirley didn't like it. She went home every other weekend and Shirley had been to visit a few times, but she had just been introduced as Rosie's friend. No-one here knew about Rosie and Shirley – apart from me now and I musn't tell anyone. But Shirley didn't like being kept secret and was threatening to end the whole thing if Rosie didn't 'come out', as it were. But – and here was the best bit – Rosie wasn't sure she wanted to come out – at least not as someone who was in a serious relationship. She still fancied other people and occasionally copped off with them. And other *people* seemed to include men.

Hurrah! The sexiest girl I had met all term was *bisexual*! This was even more the stuff of fantasy than it had been a few minutes ago. Suddenly, I thought I'd led a very sheltered life.

I woke up dying of thirst. I didn't know where the hell I was, but a bedside radio alarm said **7:14.** I was dying for a pee and had a searing headache was edging its way into my skull. Then I felt someone stir next to me.

Unlike me, Rosie had obviously undressed at some point in the night. In that post-alcohol search for sleep, she had one arm under the pillow and a leg outside the bed. She was wearing a T-shirt and a black G-string. Mascara still streaked her face, but I wasn't really looking at her face at that point.

Then she woke with a start.

I smiled. "Hi. Are you okay?"

Once again, she clearly wasn't. She pulled the covers right around her and sat bolt upright.

"Who the fuck are you?"

It was the beginning of a beautiful friendship.

6. GBH Unlimited

Lee Macken stared defiantly at the three people sharing his elevator car. The gay-looking bloke with his cufflinks, the speccy posh bird with the broach, the brain dead blonde who was probably somebody's secretary and part time shag.

He sensed the disapproval wafting out of their noses, their very skin, as he crammed his way into the elevator car, battered briefcase in hand, and punched the button for floor 12. Everybody knew there was only one company on floor 12 – Lee's own company, GBH. And all these fluttering fuckwits had protested vociferously when the office space had been leased to GBH a few weeks ago.

What was wrong with these people? Lee ran a good, honest, professional business. Where was the difference between him and them – bankers, loan sharks, credit blacklisters, lawyers? They were all the same. They saw a gap in the market and went for it. They made a good living. They scared people too, all of them. So why all the looks down noses, why the knowing exchanges of glances?

It was all wrong, this snobbery about people because they made money. In the old days, businesses like Lee's had been illegal. A huge, monolithic state had controlled everything that people did and taken most of their money off them in taxes to pay for more surveillance of their lives. Thousands of people were employed by the government simply to tell other people what to do – doctors, police, teachers, all paid for by members of the public, who were known in those days as *taxpayers*. The 'nanny state' was in complete control of everything and everyone.

Lee loved reading about the socialist era. The country had gone into a kind of collective madness after two massive wars had run it into the ground. People had become 'taxpayers' and enterprise was a dirty word. Huge socialist empires were set up – the hated Inland Revenue took money directly from people's wages to fund the vast bureaucracy, including a National Health Service that squandered billions paying for feckless people to treat illnesses they had caused themselves – it was nothing like the cutting edge NHS of today, a market leader in healthcare. Those who tried to change things, to insist that people should keep their wages to pay for their own wants and needs, were dismissed as heretics and extremists. Worse still, people who didn't earn wages at all were funded by those who did – the Inland Revenue was unashamedly socialist and would take your hard-earned money to pay for the lazy and stupid who earned nothing.

But eventually, common sense came to the fore. Politicians began to speak of a smaller state, of people taking more responsibility for themselves. Slowly, painfully, the power of the vast state was weakened. The market shocks of the early 21st century had shown that people were living beyond their means – regulation of the free market and government intervention in the economy had to stop. The first floods had helped too, in their own strange way – as more and more people got displaced, the cost of running the nanny state started to become unmanageable. With health problems rising and less people making money for the state to steal, governments had to start making cuts to the socialist empire simply to allow people enough money to keep the economy going.

And most people liked having more responsibility and more financial freedom. Once they got used to being self-sufficient, they wanted less and less socialism and a smaller and smaller state. If they wanted healthcare or education, they could buy it – as long as they didn't have to pay for others to have it as well.

Ironically, the people Lee admired most from the post-socialist era were not the great politicians who had brought about these changes in the public psyche, but the people who had made them think more radically. People who were known at that time as 'criminals' – it sounded almost as antiquated as 'taxpayer'. The smaller state had created plenty of losers, people who didn't have the money to buy designer goods, healthcare or food - and some of these people turned to activities that were illegal at the time, simply to make ends meet. Eventually, the politicians were sensible enough to realise that a small state means less money to spend chasing people around and telling them what they aren't allowed to do, so some of the lesser 'crimes' were ignored to the point where they were effectively permissible.

It had, though, taken a visionary Government to recognise that allowing people to be self-sufficient in this way was a good thing and that crime – an ugly, socialist word – was simply a way of the state interfering in people's lives.

Organisations like the Taxpayers' Federation and the even more radical Tireless Workers Against Tax had started to argue that money should not be wasted on needless things like policing, when more and more citizens were paying for their own private security – effectively paying twice. The Government agreed. In a series of Enterprise Acts – the last of them, in 2030, abolishing (or '*privatising*') most remaining crimes – they had unshackled the true enterprising spirit of the British people. Those illegal activities that remained would themselves create revenue as a new, privatised police industry would charge people for investigating them. This was the only real reason why crime still existed at all – as a way of making money.

So what was the fucking problem?

Floor 9 and two of them got out without a backward glance. Now it was just him and Blondie. She stared at the buttons as if willing the car to speed up. For fuck's sake, was he some kind of rapist or something now? Floor 11 and out she popped. Felt like she was relieved to get away from him. Daft fucking bint.

Out on to Floor 12 and into the office. Fucking tip. Malone was going to have to learn to keep the place tidier. He rummaged under a pile of papers on his desk and found the answerphone: *4 messages waiting*.

"Oh. H-hello. It's Mrs Garland here. Mrs Rowena Garland. I'm just phoning to say – well, to say thank you. A job very well done indeed. Arthur hasn't had a moment's trouble with the Jamesons since your boys talked to them. We've put another cheque in the post. I know we paid up front, but we just wanted to say thank you, for such a - marvellous job! *Thoroughly* professional! Thank you so much. Goodbye!"

There you go, Blondie. That's what we do. Protecting the community. Read the fucking strapline.

"Good morning. It's Dr Braithwaite here, St Margaret's Hospital. I'm calling about a Mr Kit Jameson. He – er – says some of your representatives have his ear. We're quite keen to know whether they kept it frozen or not, as we'd like to sew it back on. Apparently, they promised him that they would look after it for him. You can get me on 020 7777 8899. Dr Richard Braithwaite. Thank you."

Lee spluttered and grinned. *Oh sure, Dr Brain Dead, we've a freezer full of ears. Take your pick. Oh no – seems we're right out of them today. Will a nose do?* He chuckled again.

"Hey, GBH. It's Sammy here. Sammy Wonder, Sales Section at the National Health Service. I tried calling you last week, but you guys haven't come back to me. Need a bit of an old chin wag with you about how we can work together. Gimme a call, boys! Nice one!"

"Oh – er – wotcha GBH. Sammy here. NHS sales. Forgot to leave my number. It's 07102

Twenny-nine, twenny-nine, twenny-two. Call me. Yo."

What was this fucking drip on? Perhaps he should give him a call – there was no other business coming his way today. But how the fuck was he supposed to work with the Health Service? They were all about making people better, weren't they? Yeah – well, maybe there was a kind of connection, if you saw the whole thing as a kind of production line…

He picked up the phone. Better check Malone had sorted the noisy neighbours down on Lofting Road.

"Doug? It's Lee. You busy?"

"Nah. No go. Bastards are out. We're dahn the boozer."

"Well don't get pissed. I don't want you lot going too far – or not far enough. Stay in control."

He was sure Malone was suppressing laughter. "Don't worry, Boss. We're on the case. Another pint, we'll hit the road. Then we'll hit those fuckers on Lofting Road!"

"You do that. A client's paying good money to get them sorted."

"Consider it done, Boss. Over and out."

"Yeah - break a leg!"

He hung up. He never entirely trusted Malone and his gang. He'd hired them from a building site and always felt they'd taken the same laissez-faire attitude to their new jobs as they had their old. Half of East London had been half-built by Malone's old company before it went bust.

The phone rang. Not Stevie fucking Wonder from the NHS, surely? He picked it up.

"GBH Unlimited. MD speaking."

"Ah. Good morning to you, Mr Dee. Name's Rio Winstanley. From Capital Hitmen."

Lee raised his eyebrows. Then he realised that didn't work over the phone.

"You still there, Mr Dee?"

"Ah, it's Mr M, actually. Macken."

"Mr Em? I thought you said Mr Dee?"

"No. Name's Macken?"

"How many names you got, Brother? You taking the piss?"

"One name. Lee Macken."

"That's two names."

"Look, do you want something?"

"We do."

Lee sighed. *I know what you fucking want and I've got the boys to do it!*

"I'm a busy man, Mr Winstanley. What is it you want?"

"You know what our game is?"

Fuck's sake. "No, let me guess."

"Okay."

Fuck's sake! "Window cleaners?"

Now there was a big, shrieking laugh. "Window cleaners! I like your style, Mr Dee! Mr Em! I like it! Window cleaners!"

He could hear that his joke had gone down a storm with Mr Winstanley's colleagues as well. If indeed they realised it was a joke.

"Alright, can we come to the point, Mr Winstanley? Is someone bothering you? And if they are, can't you take care of it yourself?"

"Oh no. We can't do that. It's illegal. We're licensed murderers. We can't start insider dealing and contracting our own killings. You get fined for that. Or put in prison." Suddenly, Rio Winstanley sounded like some prick from the Home Office.

"So what do you want?"

"We have – a rival. Cocky bastard. Reckons he's better than us and keeps bad-mouthing my boys in the press."

"I see."

"We want this man taught a lesson. A serious lesson."

"I think I get the picture."

"Coolio. So what do I need to do next?"

"You send me an email with the details on. I fax you an invoice, you sign it and send it back. And the serious lesson is taught. What's the fella's name?"

"It's Hartley. Keith Hartley."

"It's fucking *whaat*? You've got to be fucking *kidding!* No way!"

Lee hung up the phone. Fucking jokers. His boys have a go at that maniac – it'd cost him a year's sick pay.

The phone rang again.

"Look, just fuck off! I'm not interested!"

"Wo-ah! Allow me to chat things through with you first!"

"What? Who is this?"

"It's Sammy. Sammy Wonder. Sales Section, National Health Service."

6. Murder Masterclass

"Reight. You wanna bump someone off. 'Ow do you do it?"

"How? Oh. Dunno."

Keith and I stood facing each other in his cellar. A dark, manky little room that smelled of cat piss, mould and sweat. The only other things in the room were a chair and a large box he'd struggled down the cellar steps with – which kind of scared me, given his profession. This room was his training suite, he'd informed me proudly. "An' where t' bodies are buried, if ya know worra mean!"

A shudder had run through me as I realised it may not be a figure of speech. But I felt strangely honoured when Keith told me I was the first person he'd tried to pass on his trade to. I know it gave the lie to this being any kind of regular 'training suite', but it made me feel a bit special. In fact, just being in his big house in Canonbury and still being alive felt like a bit of a privilege in itself.

"Now remember this," he'd started. "Yer nowt special. Nor am I. We're just blokes tryin' to make a livin'. Lose sight of that, and you lose everythin."

No icebreaker, then. Straight into the training. The next question was the one about how I'd kill someone. My response didn't impress.

"Ya dunno! Well, fook's sake, Fella, 'ave a bloody guess!"

I don't think I said anything.

"Well, come on! 'Ow many ways are there to kill someone? It's not bloody rocket science!"

"Oh. Ok. Poison them?"

"Ya fookin' puff! Poison 'em! What a fookin' gaylord! Why poison?"

"No blood. Easy to avoid detection. Dunno."

"'Dunno!'' 'Dunno!' he mimicked, waving his hands about in a camp way that didn't suit him at all. "Well, stick yer poison up yer arse. Gimme another!"

"Shoot them?"

Keith threw his hands up in the air. "Shoot 'em! What are you now, a fookin' cowboy?"

"Well...why not?"

"Where's the fookin' skill in that? Any arse wipe can shoot someone! Look at them girly Capital Hitmen. All guns an' rap music! Kill twenty blokes tryin' to do one! Wankers!" He spat on the ground.

"Oh. Okay."

"Okay! I'll give ya okay! Now to save me standin' ere all night, I'm gonna come to the point."

"Righto."

"If I'm gonna train ya – *against* ma better judgement, to be honest – then yer gonna 'av to get one thing straight. Killin' is a craft. It's not some fookin' paper round that anyone can do! It's a trade – and a trade that takes skill and dedication. Ya follow me?"

I nodded.

"No you don't!" he snapped back, quite correctly. "But you'll learn. I'll teach ya."

Oh God, he was trying that kindly smiling thing now. It just wasn't his game.

Killing, he explained, was an undervalued, increasingly underpaid trade. You got too many cowboys in his profession – fly-by-nights with guns and explosives, women (and 'nancy boys' like me) with poison. What they didn't have was a love of the trade, a real love of killing.

"The madness," he said, his eyes gleaming proudly. "To be real mur-derer, ya need the madness! I mean, would ya take on a plumber who knew nowt about pipes? Or a gard'ner who couldn't stand plants, but needed the money? Nah!"

What you needed was a proper tradesman who knew his craft and took pride in his work. There were just too few like him about.

"So – how do you kill your victims?"

He looked as if he'd been shot by one of the Capital Hitmen.

"You *what*? Victims!"

"Yes – sorry, is that the wrong way to-?"

"Victims! Shawn, these people are not my *victims*! They're my *wages*! My customers pay good money to 'ave 'em killed. An' properly killed, by a fookin professional! Victims! Ya make it sound like t' bad old days when this craft were a crime!"

"I'm sorry…"

"Victims! Lord sev us!" He shook his head. "Reight. Ah'll cut t't'chase. Ya wanna kill folk? 'Ere's 'ow."

And he drew a fat finger across his throat.

"Slash 'em. Slash 'em, from ear to ear. By all means stun 'em first if need be. But you want it to look reight an' you wanna be sure they're dead - it's ear to ear."

I gulped. "Ear to ear."

"Then once they're dead, you can 'av a bit o' fun. Slice 'em down the middle and fillet the fookers. Cut out their 'eart if you want to – jilted lovers like that touch. Cut their eyes out, or chop off their knob. It's up to you. Just be a tad – creative - ya follow?"

"Creative… right…"

"But don't try to be funny. It don't go down well. Don't take the piss. I 'eared of a case once where a fella 'ad 'is knob sewn on 'is bonce an' they'd drawn an 'Hitler 'tache on 'im. Not on, that. Killin's not a joke. That kind o' thing marks ya down as an amateur – or a savage. We don't want that, do we?"

"No. We don't."

"Reight. So that's yer starter for ten. Now. Practice time!"

His eyes gleamed and he reached down to the box at his feet. He'd lugged it down here when he first came in and I had worried it was his last victim - sorry, wage. Fortunately, I was wrong. Keith pulled out a lifesize doll – the kind a certain kind of lonely man blows up and has sex with. Even in 2050. And this one was fully blown up – I hoped it hadn't been used.

"Now. This 'ere's yer first practice model. She's been shaggin' around an' 'er old man wants 'er dead." He threw the doll on to the only chair in the room. "You do it. Kill 'er, Shawn!"

"Ah – what with?"

He tried the smiling again. "Good question! An' let it be a lesson to ya. I expect a good workman to turn up wi' tools. Nex' time, reight?"

I smiled. I didn't really know what else to do.

"For now, there's a carvin' knife in me kitchen. Not me meat one – use the one in the sink, that's a good 'un. Come on, Shawn, look sharp!"

I ran up the stairs. I was tempted to keep on running, to never come back. Not to Keith's house, not to London, not to the Western hemisphere. The blood was pounding in my ears and my whole body was sweating. I really wasn't sure this job was for me. But Keith scared the shit out of me and I was too scared to tell him.

And there, lying in the sink – *fuck*, I nearly fainted.

Soaking in his kitchen sink was a carving knife with a curved black handle. Its blade was caked in blood. I leaned on the sink and heaved for a moment.

Then I gritted my teeth, wiped the crap off it with a tea towel and trotted back downstairs. As I got to the bottom, I had the biggest rush of fear and desperation I'd ever felt in my life – so I sped up. By the time I reached the middle of the room, I was sprinting.

I charged right at the blow-up doll, knife outstretched and yelling.

"*Grrroooooooaaaahhh….!*

Then my foot gave way and I was sailing through the air. The knife flew out of my hand and I pitched forward, ending up face down in the blow up doll's fanny.

Keith was shaking with his aspiring laugh.

"Fookin' rubbish!" he pronounced and shook some more.

His foot was still outstretched from where he'd tripped me. Even the doll looked amused. I removed my face from its nether regions and tried to smile back. I'd clearly failed my apprenticeship. Ah well – maybe a bar job was more me anyway.

"Dodgy start, Shawn. But reight attitude. You'll learn!"

Shit.

8. The Oil Man Cometh

Betsy Saunders had a blinding headache. She sat at her desk and buried her face in her hands. It was days like these when she wondered if it was really worth it.

Socialism was just not fashionable anymore. She could try to pretend it was, but it wasn't. Her Dad had been a real old fashioned Brownite, into redistributing wealth and spending money on public services. But the march of history had not been kind to Brownism.

No-one believe in that kind of hard left stuff anymore. No-one except Betsy. Oh, sure. there was that Socialist Worker Party, the ones that were always talking about Tony Blair, Gordon Brown and the golden age of socialism, but most of them were about twelve years old. The argument for public services had been lost years ago and it was pointless trying to reverse the tide.

Even within her own party, attitudes had changed. No-one really spoke about poor people anymore, because poor people couldn't afford to register to vote. And no-one really *despised* the Enterprise Act in the way her Dad had – they just talked about the need for reform, about applying the values of people like her Dad to the modern world, which basically seemed to mean jettisoning most of the values.

Her Dad had been working as a Change Manager in the old National Health Service when the Enterprise Act came into force. He'd lost his job when it was privatised, of course, and never actually worked again in the 'New New Britain' that Cameron Blair had promised. The new National Health Service wouldn't have employed someone like him in a million years – a Change Manager fiercely opposed to change. But that wasn't the real focus of his anger.

"Privatising crime!" he would rant, night after night, as her Mum talked dirty on the phone nearby. "It's absolutely scandalous!"

Her Mum had smiled benevolently while squeezing a wet sponge next to the phone and breathing very heavily. She'd lost her job as an Infection Control Nurse too - and now she was making ends meet by pretending to be called Sasha, for a company called Bored Housewives. Betsy often wished her Mum would go to the bedroom to do her work, but her father wouldn't hear of it. "I want you working where I can see you," he said. Socialist or not, he wanted to know the work was a chore - and he certainly didn't want it going on in his bedroom.

"Amnesty for all murderers now," he announced one night. "I knew it was coming!"

The Enterprise Act of 2030 had taken the final step, legalising crimes that had previously caused public revulsion. For hundreds of years, governments had wrestled with the problems of violent crime, robbery and murder while being faced with statistics that told them more and more people were engaging in them. But the Government in 2030 was different. They talked about a 'democratic deficit', where the state was clearly out of tune with what the people wanted. They talked about finding ways of allowing people more freedoms, more responsibility for themselves and to keep more of their own money. They talked about the private and voluntary sectors doing more to support poor people or those displaced by the floods. They privatised healthcare and education and scrapped the welfare benefits that they said created a dependency culture. And finally, they said the previously unthinkable - that if people could make money from an activity, however distasteful to others, then that was almost always a good thing for the economy. Such people would be less dependent on a state that was increasingly small and powerless anyway.

They put in a couple of laws protecting politicians from being murdered or commissioning murders– it could harm the democratic process, they said, if politicians were able to kill one another – and basically made the free for all that was already emerging both legal and a central part of their own ideology.

"Outrageous!" her Dad said. "The politicians have opted out altogether. They can't stop crime, so they change its name to enterprise! And no-one bloody cares enough to stop them!"

It was true – people didn't seem to care much. They just liked not having to pay taxes for public services that clearly didn't work. Unless someone close to them was a victim, things like murder and violence were only of salacious interest. All that mattered was earning enough money to be able to feed and clothe your family and to pay for your healthcare and insurance, to live somewhere nice and high above sea level and now to protect yourself from being burgled, assaulted or murdered. This lot were just being honest – politics had never managed to stop bad things happening in spite of all the taxes and the massive state, so they may as well get all the bad things above board and regulated and helping the economy – and be allowed to keep their wages rather than have them squandered by the taxman. Sure, there were a few protests, but most people just got on with their lives, watched reality TV and planned their next holiday. Turnout at the next election stayed at about 19%.

One notorious serial killer, a psychopath named Keith Hartley, had been on the front of all the papers. He was promising to set up his own business under the new legislation. Betsy remembered how shocked her father had been that someone could openly make a living from killing people. That seemed so long ago now.

What was it all about? Here she was, 36 years old, single, increasingly lonely. Six years as an MP had achieved nothing. The tide of history stared impassively back, picking up her speeches, her campaigns, her biting sarcasm, and lobbing them back on to the beach. And every man she met seemed to be either a kiss-and-tell merchant wanting to run to the Sun with stories of shagging Britain's Looniest Leftie, or a promisingly right-on but ultimately unreliable younger man. She had no-one to talk to at night. No-one to support her, challenge her. Have *sex* with her.

A tap on the door made Betsy start. She peered out through her fingers. Ryan Blake, the Chief Whip, was sliding into her office.

"Ah, Betsy," he oozed. "Everything alright?"

She sighed and closed her fingers. "Not great. Headache."

"Oh dear. Allow me."

She peered out through her fingers again. Blake had produced a pack of Cannabis Gum from his inside pocket.

"Thanks, I don't."

"Really? How quaint. You take Aspirin?"

"I take nothing."

"I see. Understandable I suppose. They say Nothing Acts Faster Than Cannabis!" He smirked at his joke.

Betsy lowered her hands. "Is this a social call, Ryan?"

"Well – you could say that. Just checking you're okay."

"How sweet of you. I'm fine."

If Ryan were a cat, he would be rubbing around her desk now. No, forget that, he *was* rubbing around her desk.

"It's just – well, Greg is a bit – concerned about you."

"That's unusual."

He smiled awkwardly and continued to caress her desk. "No, you misunderstand him. He has a huge amount of respect for you."

"Yeah, right."

"Seriously. He's often thought about putting you in the Shadow Cabinet."

"Or a locked cabinet."

Ryan Blake laughed his oily laugh. "Very droll! Always said you had a terrific sense of humour, Betsy!"

"I also have a headache. Can we come to the point?"

"Well – like I say, Greg's a bit concerned. You don't seem yourself. I mean, that scene in the House yesterday – it wasn't good. Are you quite – well, are you quite well?"

"I'm fine. Apart from the headache."

He smiled. And hovered. He was getting oil on the carpet.

"Oh, okay Ryan! It was a crap intervention! I was bored senseless by that little prick Splash and just decided to have a pop! Not one of my better moments."

Blake's eyebrows tried to show concern, but his eyes were having none of it. "Indeed. Not one of the People's Party's finest either."

"Hard to think of any great People's Party moments. We've yet to win a single election."

"Indeed. Absolutely! And that's the nub of the gist, so to speak. I don't really know how to put this politely, Betsy. But – well, with performances like yours yesterday, we won't *ever* win an election!"

Betsy said nothing. There was a lot she could have said – it wasn't like in the Kellogs House yesterday where she lost her thread – but she couldn't be arsed to say any of it. Besides, Blake knew where she stood. A long way from him and the policies he thought would 'win an election'.

"I suppose what I am trying to say – in a nutshell – is that it wasn't really acceptable what happened. Our first concern is you and your – mental state. But we also have to keep the election in mind."

He stopped and beamed insincerely. "So – how do ya wanna play this?"

"Play what?"

"Well – do you want us to refer you to a doctor, give you a few weeks off, that sort of thing? Withdraw the whip? Discipline you?"

Betsy smiled. "Ooh, I love it when you talk dirty, Ryan!"

His smirk vanished. "Oh dear. You don't seem to be taking this matter very seriously."

"No, Ryan, I'm not taking it at all fucking seriously!" she snapped. "Because what you're saying is fucking bollocks, as per usual! Frankly, it's up to you how you 'play' things. I am elected by my constituents and I will answer to them, not you and Styles!"

"Actually, you are also elected by your constituency People's Party. From a list of candidates approved by me."

"So fire me then, you little tosser! Fire the one dissenting voice! Very democratic!"

"Betsy, I really don't think there is any need to speak to me like that. We have been good friends for several years. I came here to help you."

"We were friends until you stuck your tongue up Styles's arse and got the Whip's job. And 'friends' is putting it loosely."

Blake looked hurt. Oily pain. "I'm sorry you feel that way, Betsy. I really am."

He stood facing her, blinking ludicrously. She was *dying* to laugh. It was a great relief when, without another word, he turned on his heel and left her office. The laughter burst out then like water smashing through a dam, and she knew he'd heard it. That made her laugh louder and longer. Maybe she *was* losing it after all.

9. The Stalker Next Door

Another fucking row. Rosie didn't know if she could stand it anymore. Once, the passion and mutual dependence of her life with Shirley had seemed irreplaceable, eternal. Now it seemed to be one long argument.

So Sean came around to take the cat for a walk. Big Fucking Deal. Sean came around every other day for some spurious reason or other. He had even borrowed a bag of sugar once.

"The guy is a prize prick!" Shirley had yelled for the seventh or eighth time. "He's *dying* to get into your pants. Are you *so* easily flattered that you can't just tell him to piss off?"

"Sean and I are friends," Rosie had insisted. "And I won't have you treat him like that!"

Shirley had stormed off hours ago. It was becoming a regular thing. Rosie knew exactly where she was, in the Hope & Anchor on Upper Street. Her storms always seemed to lead her there. She'd be sitting in a corner with a pint, glowering at everyone else while casting surreptitious looks at the door. Usually, by about 11.30, Rosie would turn up and say she'd been looking for her everywhere. Shirley would spit and growl and slur her words and play hard to get. But her relief would be palpable.

Not all of their rows were about Sean, though lots of them were. Their rows were basically about anyone else who came into Rosie's life. Not just men, but anyone who Rosie seemed to hit it off with. When Rosie was a student, Shirley had always made a point of being obnoxious to her friends and trying to embarrass Rosie in front of them.

"She hasn't told you were shagging, has she? We're lezzas!"

It never worked. Mainly because, after the first few meetings, Rosie kept Shirley entirely away from her new friends. But also because Rosie had snogged a series of men in the first few weeks of Uni and no-one there seriously believed she had a female girlfriend back in Stoke. By the time she met Ben, her best friend from home wasn't someone any of her Manchester friends wanted to hang out with.

Shirley had met Sean, though. Sean had become a big fixture in Rosie's university life. The first morning she'd woken up with him, she'd been terrified. What on earth had she done – and who was this she'd done it with? Then they'd talked and she'd remembered bits of the night before. What a cringe fest that was - but what a Nice Guy.

Sean defined ordinary. He was not good looking, he was not ugly. Not fat, not thin, tallish but not strapping. Fair hair cut short, even face, standard dress. He looked like everyone else. There was something comforting about that which was impossible to explain.

It was when she got to know him properly that she realised he had mad insecurities too. At first, he'd seemed the most solid, level-headed bloke she had ever met. A great listener and someone who didn't judge. But as their friendship developed, she realised there was more to it than that. Sean, whose friendship she had come to value over almost anyone else's, was deeply infatuated with her, if not insanely in love with her.

It had probably been in Stoke that she'd seen it first, when Sean first met Shirley. Sean had come to visit her one weekend when Shirley was meant to be away on an NHS Quit Cocaine weekend. But Shirley hadn't gone. She'd got on the train, then got off again and come back to Stoke. To find a 'fucking student' in her flat. And a *male* one at that.

Shirley wasn't looking for an innocent explanation. She launched straight into a screeching fit. "Who the fucking hell is this? Is this what goes on while I'm away? I don't fucking *believe* it!"

It had taken a long while to calm her down and Sean had been exemplary. What had chilled Shirley above all seemed to be the fact that Sean knew who she was. But this didn't mean she was going to like him. After the screeching and crying had ended, they'd all gone for a drink together and Shirley seethed with hatred every time Sean spoke.

Every time he went to the toilet – and his bladder wasn't the strongest after a couple of pints – she would start. "Can't you see this guy's after you? Oh, come on! You're a walking wet dream to him! Well, I don't want to be a part of his wet dreams, thank you very much!"

As the drinking continued, her hostility became more and more open until eventually, she challenged him directly as he was bringing over the last round at about one in the morning.

"You fancy Rosie, don't you?" Shirley was nothing if not direct. Sean put the pints down carefully.

"What do you mean?"

"What do you mean, what do I mean? You want to get into my girlfriend's knickers! Don't you?"

"No."

"Don't give me that, Sean! It sticks out a mile. Your tongue, I mean!"

"Shirley, pack it in!" Rosie had wailed. But it was then she knew. Something in Sean's eyes told her Shirley had hit the nail on the head. It wasn't a look of annoyance and he was far too pissed to be embarrassed. It was something in the way he looked at her. A tenderness that was hard to bear. Like he couldn't stand it if she looked appalled at the very idea. She tried hard not to.

Eventually, Shirley did one of her storm-outs - knocking over her pint as she left. Then it was just Rosie and Sean. And part of her wished, really wished, that she fancied him back and they could just fuck off somewhere into the sunset.

"I wasn't expecting her to be jealous!" Sean said, smiling, but there was an awkwardness there. A question.

Rosie sighed dramatically. "She's jealous of anyone I talk to. It's mental!"

"And does she always accuse them of trying it on with you?"

"Sometimes."

They picked up their glasses like synchronised boozers. Drank. Put their glasses down in perfect unison.

"I hope I haven't caused a row?" he said uncertainly.

"Course not. Shirley caused it. She's mad. She's just so fucking insecure," she said and added, hating herself, "I mean, me and you. How fucking far-fetched is that?"

He laughed. And there it was, in his eyes. She had killed it softly, quietly, with the minimum of fuss, as soon as it had appeared. And there, behind his laughter, his eyes told her how crushed he was.

But they had stayed friends. They had stayed friends all through Uni, even when she met Ben. Sean had rented the flat next door to her for a while, then moved to London shortly after she did - and ended up her neighbour again, renting the flat across the hall.

"It's called stalking!" Shirley used to say, and maybe it was. But Sean was so much more than a stalker. He was her best friend, the one person who really seemed to understand her, really seemed to care about her feelings. So what if he was sometimes- awkward, even deranged, in her presence. He listened to her when no-one else would. He would always be there for her. And he didn't scare her like Shirley sometimes did.

Rosie ran her fingers through her hair. 11.15. She should be heading for the Hope & Anchor now. But it was raining outside and she was still angry. Maybe she should wait an hour, make Shirley really sweat. No, fuck it. Don't play games. She went into the bedroom, opened the wardrobe and pulled on her jacket. The pocket vibrated, then her phone rang loudly. Maybe Shirley was going to make up with her this time – that would be a first.

She pulled out her phone. It was Ben. He was not smiling. It never rained but it poured.

10. Thinking of England

Richard Splash lay back and thought of England. Not the England that women of generations past had supposedly dreamt of as their husbands pounded away ineffectively. The England he and others like him had created.

The England of opportunity for all, of free enterprise, gargantuan profits, no crime. He and his ilk had changed Britain forever, made it once again the finest country in the world. Only in this England, this utopia, would a man of his standing mix so easily with a slut like the bitch who was currently sucking his penis. Free enterprise was a great leveller. She had her needs and he had his. And she'd been taking care of them for nearly an hour – mainly because he'd earlier ordered a wrap of finest cocaine from Elite, *Druggists for the Discerning*. He wasn't sure how much longer this would go on, but who cared. He'd paid good money for it.

Sadie from Whores 4 U was getting jaw ache. Hard to believe, as this greasy little cock was the tiniest she had ever seen. She really hadn't believed they came in miniature until she met this posh, ugly little runt. And now she was wondering if miniatures came at all. She'd been trying every trick she knew to make the little shit blow his load. Nothing seemed to work. He kept lying back, sighing, thrusting, then seeming to drift away. It was bloody uncomfortable. She felt like biting the end off just to get a reaction.

What an honour it was for this little nobody to be sucking him off. He, Richard Splash, Minister for Free Enterprise. The rising star of a glorious country. And a girl who couldn't afford the same school, getting to nibble Ole Percy. She'd be telling her grandchildren in years to come that she'd had the Prime Minister's dick in her mouth. No, he didn't think that was too far fetched. He was going to the top. Ole Percy was coming too. All in good time, of course.

She was sure she'd seen this bloke on the telly. He was a politician or a GBH salesman or something. Little prick, in more ways than one. Treated her with a disdain, an arrogance, you just didn't expect from customers. Ok, he'd paid his money up front, but there was something really rude about the way that he'd just unzipped and said "Suck it". He could have asked to see the menu and asked for number 3, like most normal customers. Weirdo.

It had been another glorious day and this was a good way to end it. A few lines and a cut-price whore. Richard preferred the cheaper whores. These so called high class ones wanted to have a conversation, wanted to make out that there was some element of foreplay, of consent. That you'd met on some kind of blind date and just ended up having sex. That wasn't the way Richard liked it at all. These strange girls that faked orgasms, asked about your family and your job. No, he preferred the cheaper option when it came to slappers. Not the downtown types, not the illegal ones either – just the bog standard, run-of-the-mill Whores 4 U types, who were usually quite pretty and just delivered the goods in that pleasant, straightforward way, like Asda selling you washing powder. A nice smile, a fairly mean tip, and off you went home.

When was this fucking arsehole going to come? It'd been over an hour now, must have been. This was costing her time, and time was money. The taste and smell of his sweat was making her gag and still he showed no sign of climaxing. And – now what the fuck was he doing? The cheeky fuck had only leaned over for the remote and switched on the telly! It'd cost her a tenner of his fee, that, and the pay per view rates were rocketing as he leaned back and sighed pathetically again.

Ah, the Parliament Channel. What a way to relive his moment of glory. That brainless bitch Betsy Saunders was going through the motions. She was off her face. Bet she wished she was on his! Imagine that…strange bedfellows indeed! No, really. Imagine. Betsy *fucking* Saunders!. The last living socialist. *Betsy* bloody *gorgeous*-dirty-lefty-*frigging-fucking-Betsy….fuck*! Little fucking lefty fucking lovely little – if this was….*ohhhhhhhh*!

To Sadie's great relief, the TV seemed to have done the trick. Watching MPs making boring speeches got this sad fucker off. She gagged again as the sweaty little member's sweaty little member slid frantically in and out of her mouth. Then with one last, puny gasp, he was done. Fucking loser.

"Well, thank you Ada. That was magnificent!"

Then, with a sheepish grin and unexpected force, Richard Splash punched Sadie full in the mouth, breaking two of her teeth. "Slut!" he spat. Then he pulled on his clothes and left her lying there, bleeding and in tears.

11. Customer service

"The only way to learn is to shadow the best. Come out on a job wi' me."

I'd been working for Keith for six weeks when he first mooted my lack of progress as a murderer. While his office was spotless, his leaflets were superbly desk top published and his books were in better order than ever before, he didn't feel I was quite "gettin' there" on the killing front.

"I didn't take you on to keep me shop tidy an' ave nice telephone manners. Why aren't you itchin' to take on a job?"

Truth was, my experience in Keith's cellar with the sex doll had all but convinced me I wasn't cut out for killing. I'd sort of kept my head down on that front ever since. Contracts came in virtually every day and I just passed them to Keith. I knew there was no question at all of him asking me to do one on my own – but it was clear he'd at least expected me to want to accompany him a few times. He was disappointed - and I think a bit bewildered.

I'd hoped to get away with making this the most efficient and customer-friendly murder business in London. Smiling assassins, I'd thought of suggesting as a strapline. But I knew Keith didn't go in for straplines, considering them to be the work of puffs.

There is so much to do in any job if you really look for it - and especially if you are trying to avoid doing the job itself. My montage of letters of thanks from Keith's satisfied customers now hung on the newly decorated wall, Keith had state-of-the-art leaflets and a vastly improved website. People who called to arrange to have someone bumped off had never had it so good.

"Good morning, Keith Hartley Mass Murderer, Sean speaking, how may I help?"

"Oh. H-hello. I er – want someone to kill my husband."

"Great! Well, that's what we're here for. If you could just email me over the details – and any special requirements – I'll put everything in place for you."

"Special requirements?"

"There's a full list on our website. We can behead him, mutilate various body parts, torture him, pretend to let him escape – almost anything you require."

"I see."

"There's a full price list for all extras on the website. Or if you just want a straight killing, we can do that as well. Whatever you want."

"Erm – I think I'd like you just to do it. No special requirements."

"Ok. You're sure?"

"I think so."

"Any special words you'd like us to say to him first?"

"Oh. I never thought of that. Yes please."

"A special message. Lots of our customers take that option. It's fifty pounds extra, though."

"That's ok. Just say 'This is from Stella, you cheating cunt!' Is that ok?"

"Of course it is. Just pop it all in an email, together with your husband's details and where we might find him, and I'll action that straight away. Do you have a particular day on which you'd like us to kill him?"

"Oh. How thoughtful! Actually, there is. He's due to meet his girlfriend on Tuesday. It's her birthday – her eighteenth."

"Oh dear. Well, I get the picture. I'm sure it can all be arranged. If you email me over the details of where they are likely to be, we can see to it. Would you like us to do the two of them at once? We have a 'Two for one' deal just now – it's very popular in cases like yours…"

"Oh, no. I couldn't do that. She's just a kid. She used to babysit for my son. No, just him. Let her learn her lesson, but don't kill the poor kid."

"Ok – you're the boss. If you email over the details via the website, I'll email you back an invoice. As soon as you pay that, we'll name the day. It's obviously a bit extra if you want a specific day."

"That's fine. And how will I know you've killed him?"

"Well, for another ten pounds, we can text you. Otherwise, you won't hear from us unless there's a problem – and that has never actually happened with Keith Harley Mass Murderer before!"

"Ok. That's wonderful! A text would be great."

"Ok, that's fine. Is there anything else I can help you with today?"

"No. I'll email you right away."

"That's great. Thank you very much for your call and your custom. Have a lovely day now!"

I really should've gone into telesales.

But Keith was having none of me being his backroom boy. He had taken on an apprentice and now he wanted to see him deliver.

"Reight. Next Friday. The Johnson job. Obnoxious boss, employee wants him bumped off when 'e's workin' late. No-one else there and we'll 'ave a key. Yer comin' wi' me, Shawn."

It brooked no argument. If I wanted to keep my job, I was going to have to shadow the mass murderer. And the thought terrified me. But wasn't this what I'd always wanted – to be less ordinary, to live a life that had a bit of danger about it?

"Wow, how exciting!" gushed Rosie when I told her. I wasn't really meant to tell people my job because of its nature, but as I've already explained, Rosie was special – and it was hardly worth getting a glamorous job if I couldn't use it to impress her.

"Exciting? Yeah, I suppose." I was trying to do blasé cool. You know, like watching someone get hacked to death was all in a day's work and a bit of a chore.

It didn't work.

"You're not too keen, are you?"

I tried to shrug and tried to look nonplussed. That didn't work either.

"I guess it's scary on one level - and probably a bit gory!" she mused. "But Keith Hartley's a living legend. The first professional murderer in London. It's not often you get to watch a real craftsman at work. And once he's shot the guy, it'll be all over."

"Oh, he doesn't shoot people. He cuts throats."

Rosie wrinkled her nose. "Euurgh. I'd be sick if I saw that! Why not just shoot them? Much easier."

"He doesn't think like that."

She screwed up her face again. "And will you be expected to cut throats one day as well?"

"I'm not sure. I am meant to be an apprentice. Maybe I'll just sort of caddy for him. I don't know."

I *did* know. I knew Keith wanted me to take on some of what he called "the shitty little boring jobs". But I didn't want Rosie to see me as some kind of axe murderer, even if I was about to become one. I wanted her to say it was exciting like she had at first.

"Well – let me know how it goes. Sounds amazing."

Other people's jobs always do. I'd much rather be dressing as a giant needle and getting into Stamford Bridge free, as Rosie had done the previous evening with British American Heroin. But if I was going to progress in my chosen career, I had to bite the bullet. Or carry the knife, at least.

12. Coke break

Rosie passed the small wrap to Judy, who opened it up, tipped some white powder on to the window ledge and started to mash it up with her credit card. They were standing outside their offices at British American Heroin – an impressive, glass domed structure, with 200 floors and the famous revolving restaurant on top. The MD, Howard Clarke, had banned cocaine in the office because he thought it created the wrong impression and stopped people working. So coke breaks such as these had become the norm.

"So what did you do this weekend?" Judy asked as she leant over the window ledge, rolling up a twenty pound note.

"Not much." Rosie didn't want to say that she'd actually spent the weekend splitting up with her long-term partner. Her colleagues didn't know she even had a long term partner, let alone that said partner was female. Most of them knew about Ben and a couple of them had met him a few times.

"Has Ben still not moved any nearer?"

"Nah." It had become a peculiar feature of Rosie's double life that all her friends thought she was desperate for Ben to move to London and into her flat. Had he attempted to, of course, he would now be swinging from an Islington lampost and Rosie wasn't sure she wouldn't be, too. The traumas of the weekend – from when Shirley had eventually crept meekly back into the flat, wearing her fear and desperation on her sleeve, to the tearful accusations, the screaming, the broken crockery, the broken *heart* – would have been a delight in comparison.

"Awww. You're such a lovely couple as well."

Rosie said nothing. Girls like Judy always wanted people to be moving in together, getting married, having a baby. If you were single, she wanted you to meet someone new. Poor Gary, the new press officer, was plagued every week with questions about his seemingly non-existent love life. "What did you do this weekend? Where did you go? Meet anyone?" Poor fella was going to invent an imaginary girlfriend soon.

Judy was one of those people who thought her life was perfect and that everyone else aspired to it. PA to the MD of one of the biggest companies in the world. Married with two kids, one boy and one girl. Four or five glam holidays a year, personal stylists for everything from her nails to probably her pubes. And she thought it was all dead easy. You went for a job and you got it. You met a bloke and he fell in love with you. You got pregnant the first time you tried. People who didn't have lives as perfect as she thought hers was, just weren't trying hard enough.

"How was Stamford Bridge the other night? Meet any hunky footballers?"

"No. We just did our thing on the pitch at half time. There were some freaks from the NHS there as well, booing us. They were leafleting the crowd. It was a bit crap really."

Having done their lines, they sauntered back inside the building. The huge billboard advert inside the main reception area reflected the company's latest, award-winning campaign: CAN YOU HANDLE IT? Sales were rocketing, in spite of the do-gooders. Rosie felt she'd played a part in something really successful – which wasn't how she was feeling about any other part of her life.

As she got into the lift with Judy, a small balding man got out, pushing rudely past them with his briefcase.

"Oy!" shouted Judy. "That bloke is so ignorant!"

"Who is he?"

"Jake Johnson. Used to work here years ago, then went off to set up his own poxy LSD company. It's bombed. He's always back here, trying to use his old contacts to get back in the door. Howard hates him – says he's the least likeable man on the planet, ha ha!"

Howard himself was a contender for that title – a fat, joint-puffing man in his early sixties who liked to think of himself as a bit of an eccentric, rather than just a bit of a wanker. But it wouldn't do to say that to Judy, who worshipped the ground the fat twat walked on.

"Bye then!" Judy flashed her perfect grin and got out of the lift, back to her perfect desk and perfect job.

Rosie leaned back on the wall of the lift, feeling the effects of the weekend more than the coke. She had loved Shirley so much once. Why had it been so easy to tell her to go? To smash into smithereens the heart of someone who adored her, with cold words about having no feelings left? Even when she had cried, she had been in control, composed. Even when Shirley had dropped to her knees, begging her for another chance, one more try, she had felt nothing.

So what next? Meet someone else? Another woman? Another man? Move Ben into her place as Judy and the others wished she would? It all felt flat. Whatever she thought about wishing for didn't seem worth wishing for. Maybe her heart was broken, too.

13. The killing of Jake Johnson

You wouldn't think that lying face down across your boss's desk, being taken roughly from behind, could get boring. It could be dirty, guilty or insane, but surely never dull. Unless you'd done it thirty odd times and the little shit still wouldn't so much as buy you a drink outside the office.

Marianne was bored. Bored of her job, bored of her life, bored of Jake Johnson and his predictable across the desk fucks. *Oh, Jake, aren't you the big guy?* Your business is going down the tubes, your wife has run away with a Sex Tourism salesman. And still you think that laying your desperate secretary across your invoice-coated desk represents some kind of success.

On the floor, she could read a final demand from Dodge Loans Limited and a crawling letter in response from the Lothario behind her.

"Dear Mr Butcher,

As Managing Director of LSDealers, I am writing to ask for a little more time to pay off the loan of £70,000 agreed with your company. I must confess that I had somewhat under-calculated both the rate of interest and the rate at which LSDealers would grow. I am very sorry and plead with you not to involve GBH Unlimited as suggested. I had not realised that you were so closely connected to them.

If you agree not to involve them, I am sure that another arrangement can be made. Obviously, I will agree to pay the debt at the 800% interest now proposed, but alongside this, I am willing to offer whatever services you feel may be helpful. I know, for instance, that you have certain inclinations which, whilst I do not personally share..."

Fucking hell! She closed her eyes and stopped reading.

Then a crash behind her made her jump out of her skin and spin round. A young bloke was standing gormlessly in the doorway as Jake ruthlessly chucked her aside and tried to zip up.

"Er – hi."

"Who the *fuck* are you? Get the fuck out of my office!" blustered Jake.

Marianne tried half-heartedly to cover herself up as she rolled off the desk, but dignity was long gone.

The young bloke stood in the doorway self-consciously. He'd gone bright red. Poor guy.

Then suddenly, he opened his jacket and brandished a carving knife.

"Jesus H Christ!" yelled Jake, leaping back. As Marianne screamed.

But the bloke was no killer. He just looked too *ordinary*. And the knife was shaking.

Jake cottoned on quickly. In a matter of seconds, he had crossed the room, wrestled the knife out of the lad's hands and had him by the throat against the wall.

"Right, you little fucking *shit*!" he spat. "You're fucking *dead*!"

The kid looked terrified. In spite of herself, Marianne found herself feeling sorry for him. "Leave him, Jake – let him go," she said.

A broad northern voice came from the back of the room. "Yeah. Let 'im go, Jake."

Jake's fist paused in mid air as a huge man stepped out of the shadows. Then his face fell like a sinking stone. He let go of the ordinary bloke and stared at the colossus.

"Rubbish effort, that, Shawn," drawled the big bloke. "Fookin' 'ilarious!"

Jake continued to stare, still holding the knife. "Wh-what's going on?"

"Name's Keith Hartley. Mass mur-derer. This is my tray-knee. An' that's my knife." He stretched out his hand.

"I know who you are," babbled Jake, backing away and still holding the knife. "I just don't know why you're here. Not that Dodgy Loans lot, is it?"

"Nah. Disgruntled employee. Now gimme the knife, lad."

"No fucking way! You've come here to kill me! No fucking way!"

Marianne had been stunned into silence until now. Now she understood.

Now she screamed at the top of her voice.

In one movement, Keith Hartley had filled the space between them and slapped her hard across the face. She crumpled and fell to the floor.

Jake, gallant as ever, made a run for it. He ran with the knife ahead of him, straight at the young bloke blocking the doorway, who obligingly stepped aside. Then Hartley seemed to fly through the air, rugby tackling him to the ground. The briefest of struggles later, Hartley was standing over her boss, holding the knife.

"Reight. Luv. You'd best be on yer way," he said to her. "You've 'ad yer last oats off this one."

Marianne stumbled to her feet, in a daze. Jake was lying on the floor, the knife at his throat, his eyes bulging and sweat covering his face. He looked beyond terror. And a tear was trickling out of the side of one eye. He stared at her, pleading…

But there was nothing she could do. And she didn't *care* enough. She guessed it was Daniel who'd arranged all this. And the way Jake treated Daniel, she wasn't surprised. With one last look at

Jake's bulging face, she stumbled towards the door. The ordinary bloke even smiled nervously.

"You fucking *bitch*!" Jake screamed after her.

She just knew he thought it was her. Surely Daniel would've sent a card or something?

Then the door was closed, then she was in the lift.

Then she fainted.

14. The vote of confidence

It was like all my hangovers had come at once. Head in the toilet for about five hours, blood in the puke, blood in my mind. Blood on my *hands*.

Ok, Keith had done the actual slashing – much to his chagrin – but I'd been there, an accomplice. I'd seen Jake Johnson plead for his life, in tears. I'd smelt him shit himself as Keith towered over him. *Smiling*. Fucking *smiling*, as he held a man down and slashed his throat from ear to ear. Then the sickening gurgling noise, the grotesque look on Johnson's features afterwards, the passed out woman in the lift, Keith's almost apologetic kindness towards her, ordering her a taxi and waiting with her– it all seemed like a bad dream.

Then Keith had bawled me out. I mean, *really* bawled me out. What I'd just done was "totally unacceptable" and I thought he was going to slash me from ear to ear too.

"*Cowardice* is the vilest fookin' crime, Shawn!" he ranted. "The *vilest*! A hangin' offence in my book! And you fookin' bottled it tonight and that's fookin' shit! I will *not* accept cowardice in my bisniss! I will *not*!"

This went on for well over an hour. I could say very little in mitigation and was a bit too scared to try. I just sat there in the office, head bowed, trying to look for some filing I hadn't got round to doing. There was none. Still, at least he'd realised I wasn't made of the right stuff.

Hadn't he? He'd stopped shouting…

"But I can see it's 'urtin' ya. I can see that. That's the reason I'm not firin' ya tonight."

Oh…

"You want it, don't ya, Shawn? Ya wanna be the best. Ya don't wanna be a creepin' little puff! That's why yer 'ere. I *know* that! I won't give up on ya yet!"

Oh shit, he was trying to smile again.

His theory of where it all went wrong – apart from me being a bottling little college kid puff who had no balls – was that his presence had upset me. *Upset* me? His presence had saved my fucking *life*.

"You've seen now what a job is like. They don't all come quietly. An' if we're killed doin' a job, that's tough shit. Yer allowed to defend yerself against a mur-derer. No-one gets done for killin' a killer. That's what the NUM keep's bleatin' about, but to me it's fair enough. All's fair in luv an' murder."

"NUM?"

"National Union o' Mur-derers. 'Nother bunch o' right-on puffs. You'd prob'ly get on well." He tried to smile with gruff affection then, I think – another new departure he hadn't quite grasped.

"Nah. If that little twat 'ad killed ya, I'd've said fair play to 'im . 'E were only tryin' to defend 'imself after all."

So I wasn't being sacked, then. Shit and double shit.

"So – what's the disciplinary process then? Do I get a verbal warning?"

Keith spluttered. "Oh aye! Written one too if ya like. Fook's sake, when are you goin' to stop being such a little nancy? Diss- ip-linary process! My fookin' eyes!"

Keith had a better plan, much worse than any verbal warning.

"Whaddya do when a kid falls off a bike? Take it off him? Leather the fooker for not takin' care o' it? Nah. Ya put the little sod back on there. Only way to learn.

"Next time, we'll give you a nice easy job. Bein' 'onest, I thought ya might fook up the Johnson one. Nasty piece o' work, 'im. I'll give ya a nice easy one, an' ya can do it on yer tod. Once you've one under yer belt so to speak, you'll be grand."

"I'm really not sure, Keith."

"I know yer not. But put it this way, Shawn. You wanna be a mur-derer. Mur-derers kill people. It's what we *do*. An' you're not gonna make it unless you start doin' what I pay ya for."

"Actually, I'm not sure I do want to be a murderer anymore."

"Bollocks! Don't give up on yer dreams, Lad. I know how much you want it. You just need more balls. An' if I'm not there to bail you out, you'll 'ave to do it. Kill - or be killed!"

And for some reason, he shook with laughter.

And I was still shaking too, the next day. Leaning over the toilet, shaking. Too scared to quit, too scared – and, I realised, probably too much in love with Rosie - to do a runner. As I thought about the two together – the conjunction of my feelings about last night and what was to come and how I felt about Rosie, I think I actually puked up the very balls Keith said I didn't have.

It was not a good day. *I am becoming less ordinary*, I told myself. *It's bound to be hard at first*. But when I looked in the mirror, the sick-stained face that stared back looked more ordinary than ever.

15. A constituent complains

The blonde, pretty woman rolled up the ten pound note Betsy had lent her and leaned over the table. She snorted slowly, then looked up, her eyes still full of tears.

"Is that better?" Betsy said, smiling gently.

Back in her constituency office, Betsy came into her own. This was when she remembered why she loved being an MP. People came to her with problems and she provided a good ear. Ok, the state of the nation often meant she couldn't do a lot to help, but they seemed to appreciate her trying. And listening.

"So you were saying. You lost your job?"

The girl sniffed. "Yeah. I got the sack. Whores 4 U. They give me the boot."

Betsy sighed inwardly. "Really? Why?"

"Well. This punter came in. I spent ages with him. Give him a right good suc…well, you know. Spent ages. Then when he'd finished – in my mou – well, when he'd finished … he just – hit me."

For the first time, the woman raised her head as she said this. Her pretty face was ruined when she opened her mouth. The two front teeth were missing.

"I see. And he hadn't – paid to do this?" Betsy hated asking the question, but she'd been caught out like that before.

The woman looked affronted. "No way! I don't do specials. Just straight down the line. He paid up front and he didn't offer any extra. Just called me a slut and walked out!"

"And the company were no help?"

"Well, they were at first. Said it's like, totally out of order. Way out of order, they said. Talked about calling in Police UK. Then they realised who the bloke was."

"Who he was?"

The woman sneered gappily. "One of your lot. You probably won't care, I know you all stick together."

Betsy frowned. "I most certainly do care! You're saying he was a Member of Parliament?"

"Yeah. So once they found that out, they said it hadn't really been working out. Give me my cards. Said they didn't want no trouble with a Cabinet minister."

"A minister? May I ask…er…?"

"You want to know his name, don't you? Well, I'll tell you – but first I want to know what you're going to do about it." The tears were welling up again.

"Well. This man has committed an offence. It's an unlicensed assault. If he's in the Cabinet and this becomes public, he should be sacked – though you never know with this lot. But remember the Government's own strapline is *Decent Values* – they blather on all the time about being nice people in their personal lives. Plus the fact that you should actually be able to have him prosecuted."

"I can't. I've no money. Even Crown Prosecutions and Police UK are too pricey."

"I see. That's terrible. It really is. That's this Government for you." This was a line that Betsy recited to roughly nine and a half out of ten visitors to her surgery.

"So – there's nothing you can do, is there?" The sacked whore bowed her head.

"You would need to start the process within two weeks to prosecute him. How soon can you get another job?"

"Not very, in my trade. Look at the state of me."

Betsy leaned over and patted her hand, mainly because she didn't know what else to do. The woman surprised her by smiling through her tears.

"If I told you his name, could you like – shake him up a bit? Ask questions in the House, that kind of thing? I just want the bastard to suffer really."

Aha. Now we were getting to the real reason for this visit. This woman wasn't as stupid as she pretended.

"I don't know. I'm in enough trouble in the House already, to be honest."

Then Sadie played her trump card.

"His name's Richard Splash."

Betsy found herself smiling.

16. The serial heartbreaker

"What the fuck are you doing here?"

Rosie stared in disbelief at the familiar face on her doorstep. And in some horror at the holdall at his feet and the rucksack on his back.

Ben smiled. "Come on, Rosie. You can't hide away forever."

Before she could stop him, he'd crossed the threshold into her flat.

"Ah, what a lovely cat! Hello pussycat!"

"That's Timmy."

"Hello, Timmy! Awww!"

Rosie followed Ben into her living room.

"Ben – what's going on?"

Ben turned around.

And now he wasn't smiling anymore.

They stared at each other for a few moments. Then Ben took off his rucksack – and threw it violently across the room.

"*Ben*, what the fuck are you - ?"

"Shut up, Rosie!" he snapped. "Just shut up!"

Slowly, he sat down on the sofa. Rosie continued to hover in the doorway. Ben sat down, his head in his hands.

Then he started to cry. Big, heaving sobs racked his stocky body. His hands shook as he sat there.

"Hey - would you like a cup of tea?"

"Fuck off with your tea!" he sobbed.

"Ben, will you tell me what's going on?"

More sobs. Now Rosie was getting annoyed.

"Look, this isn't on! You turn up here unannounced, all your stuff with you – I mean – what *is* this?! I don't under-!"

Suddenly Ben was on his feet. "*You* don't understand! *You* don't understand! Fucking *hell*, Rosie! What about ME?!" He was bellowing now and gesticulating wildly. Tears still streamed down his face.

Rosie backed away. She had never, ever seen her cool boyfriend behave like this. Come to that, she'd never seen anyone behave like this. Probably not even Shirley, and she was off her head.

"Please, Ben! Just tell me what's going on."

Ben sighed and it came out as a low moan. Christ, he was laying it on thick, whatever it was.

"I decided," he said, his voice all broken, "That it was time we moved on. I've been asking people about it for months and they all said the same thing. 'Rosie thinks you're not serious about her. You have to show her that you are.'"

A bitter laugh escaped him. "So today was gonna be the day, as Oasis 3 might say. Come to London. Bring my stuff. The grand romantic gesture! Tell you I was staying with you. Ask you to marry me."

Rosie's head was spinning. "*Marry* you? What? But – when did I ever - ?"

"You were always so cool. Like we were still just mates. Mates who shagged each other occasionally. Less and less occasionally. And I just thought – well, everyone thought – it was a bit weird. That I didn't even have your address down here."

"But we were fine. Weren't we?"

"Nah. *You* were fine. Rolling around down here in your lesbian love nest!"

Shit!!!

How the *fuck* had he found out???

He was smirking now, in a quivery sort of way. She didn't want to say it, but it was deeply unattractive.

"You want to know how I got your address? I looked up an old mate of yours. Still had the same email address."

He was pausing for effect now. Sooner or later, guilt tripping loved ones becomes a bizarre kind of fun to the embittered.

She said it for him. "Shirley."

"Yes. Shirley. Your fucking pervy partner of five years! And of course, she was very surprised to hear from me! Told me yes, bring all my stuff here, said it would be a lovely surprise for you! It was what you'd always dreamed of! Even asked her to meet her first in the Hope and Anchor so I could be there when I told you! Oh yeah – broke it to me very gently, did your fucking girlfriend!"

Sweet Jesus. If Ben was in this state, Shirley didn't bear thinking about.

" Is she – was she - ?"

"Spare us the guilt. She was every bit as vindictive and horrible as I'd remembered the one time we met. She spun me along for an hour, till she was pissed enough to tell me. Then she gave it to me with gusto. Left nothing out. Said she was the victim in all this."

Rosie stared at her boyfriend – unrecognisable from the chilled out, witty guy she had fallen in love with. She was breaking – no, she had *broken* – another heart. They were suddenly smashing all around her like cheap crockery. But could anyone feel as wretched as she did?

"Ben, I am so, so sorry."

He shook his head.

"Words. Words, Rosie. Coming from you, words don't mean a thing. *Nothing* means anything."

Rosie was crying. She couldn't think of anything to say. And words meant nothing coming from her anyway. When had she become this vile person that was being reflected in Ben's deep brown eyes? Somehow, between them, Ben and Shirley had concocted a monster for her to become. It wasn't her. How had all this shit happened?

Ben picked up his rucksack. "I tried to hold it together, you know. To see if – if I went through with my original plan and tried to forget about it – you'd – well, I couldn't. I just couldn't. Once I saw your face, I just – nothing."

He gulped back more tears as he swung the rucksack on to his shoulder.

"Thanks for wasting my time, Rosie. And sort your fucking head out!"

And he was gone.

17. The hearing

Betsy Saunders surveyed the sorry specimens before her and sighed inwardly. Not one of the people on this panel was likely to listen to reason – or to understand it if they did.

Jock Henderson was the Chair of the People's Party. He prided himself on his fierce People's Party credentials – they said the grandfather on his Mum's side had been a pro-striking trade unionist in the old days and his father had been a tough PR consultant. Henderson was a bit of a throwback in style, going for that old firebrand-style delivery, but politically, he had long since sold his balls to the party machine.

Lucy Hammersmith had been chair of the National Union of Students a few years ago, so God knows how she'd ended up in the People's Party rather than the Coalitionists, who the NUS was affiliated to. A small, dumpy little cow in her late twenties, she was now a party whip and boy did she love the ounce of power she thought this gave her.

Ben Hill was Shadow Minister for Enterprise – Richard Splash's Commons adversary. Hill was a former party spin doctor who'd been given one of the few safe seats left at the last election and then promoted beyond his ability. He was a fat, balding man in his fifties, with a reputation for making dinner party guests howl with his sexist jokes. All ironic, he had assured Betsy in the past, while looking down her top.

And Ryan, her esteemed 'old friend', was there too – smiling in his inimitable oily way.

"So, Betsy. You've heard Ben's views. You know our views. What do you have to say?"

"Very little, to be honest. My intervention in the House was a shambles. But it was a one-off. I don't think you should be bringing my political views in to it."

Henderson's contrived gruffness was in full swing. He thumped the table.

"Betsy, this hearing is *aboot* yer political views! It's aboot the fact that you keep denooncing party policy!"

"Well, Ben's case seems to be about the intervention I made the other week with Splash."

"That was just one example! It's happening every turn-aroond. Every time I log on the net, there you are! *Betraying* this parr-ty!" Henderson thumped the table again, his face reddening.

Betsy smiled. "I didn't know I was so famous."

Henderson glowered as Lucy Hammersmith stepped in with her irritating, clipped voice. "Your attitude's doing you no favours here, Betsy. What we want is your assurance that you'll stick to party policy."

"Well, I was elected by the constituents of Islington North saying the kind of things I've said all my life. If we're talking about betrayal, I think I'd be betraying them if I said one thing to get elected, then said something else once I got in."

"You were elected on a list system. Islington North just drew the short straw!" quipped Hammersmith, smiling at Blake as she did so. To her obvious horror, the oil man was not amused. He scowled slightly and then stretched out his hands in what looked like a plea.

"Look, Betsy," he said. "You're a great parliamentary character. An intelligent, passionate woman. You can be a great asset to this party." Hammersmith looked briefly grief-stricken. "But you're biting the hand that feeds you. You can't retain the party whip when all you do is go around slating our policies. Surely you can see that?"

Ah Ryan, so plausible and reasonable.

Such a twat.

"So what do you want me to say? That I support the Enterprise Act? That our founding principles are outmoded and extreme? That sort of rubbish? Because I can't. Not only because I don't believe it, but because no-one would believe *me*!"

"That is parr-ty policy, for Christ's sake!" thundered Henderson.

"If you want me to say those things, you will have to expel me."

"Betsy!" oozed Ryan. "Nobody wants that. What we want is for you to fulfil your potential. Do you think Jock here always supported the principles of free enterprise? Of course not. Have you ever heard him making an impassioned plea for more liberal murder laws? No. But nor do you hear him say – and I quote – that the Enterprise Act is a *load of crap.*"

"I think Ryan is giving you a way out, Betsy Darling," said Hill. "Just – stay away from my brief and concentrate on some things we all agree on for a while?"

Darling indeed. His brief. The thought of Hill's enormous briefs filled her mind for a moment and she stifled an urge to giggle.

"Is something funny, Betsy?" snapped Hammersmith.

"No. Not at all. Have we done now?"

Ryan looked at her intently. "Can we take that as an undertaking that you will try to act more responsibly? Along the lines I suggested?"

"You can take it as a promise that in the next few weeks, I will be working bloody hard to advance the cause of this party and to cause trouble for the Coalitionists."

"Ah. Now that's the Betsy we know and love!"

"So - you're not giving me the boot, then?"

"No, no. That was never the intention. Not this time, anyway. But please do take heed of what we have said. Not everyone is as patient as I am."

Ryan beamed. Hammersmith and Henderson glowered. Hill stared at her tits.

18. Eastbourne under sea

Howard Clarke swept into the room, puffing his fat joint as ever.

"Ok, people. This is a major scale disaster. We have people dead, people homeless, people missing and people drowning as we speak. It's a major disaster! And what does that mean?"

The eight people in the room – Rosie and her boss Ewan, four members of the PR team and two of the directors – stared back at him. Howard didn't like his rhetorical questions answered.

"It means money, my friends! Lots of it! Get your do-gooder heads on, because we're going to sponsor the rescue mission! And that means we're *socially responsible*. And that means – " he thumped the table – "MONEY! Get in there!" He clenched his fist like a footballer who had just scored a goal and thrusted his hips against the desk.

The directors led a short round of applause and Ewan had to nudge Rosie to make her join in. Sometimes, she felt ashamed to be working for British American Heroin.

She'd cried when she'd seen the news this morning. Those poor people who had insisted it was safe to carry on living in Eastbourne, four years after the last floods. She knew Sean's parents had moved out then and gone to live in Spain, but was his little sister still there? She'd have to ring him later.

The scale of the disaster was hard to believe, though they'd been predicting it now for several years. The whole of Eastbourne was basically off the map, submerged under the raging sea. It was the first UK coastal town to formally be declared dead. The storms were expected to continue for another week at least and neighbouring areas were on red alert. Thousands of people were dead or missing – and even those who'd seen it coming in the flooding in earlier weeks and fled had lost their homes and everything in them.

"I won the contract this morning!" bragged Howard. "Those Greenpeace smoothies were trying to get it, but everyone knows how they messed up in the Falklands. All sharp suits and no sense of drama! Well, let me tell you, we're going to run one of the most spectacular, newsworthy operations this country has ever seen! There won't be a dry eye in the house – if that's, ah, the right term to use under the circumstances!"

The room erupted in laughter. One of the directors was already wiping tears from his eyes.

"So what I want is this. Press release today – on my desk in five. Rescue teams in this afternoon – use someone like Larry's Lifeboats, they're cheap as chips. Get Fire Fire on the case too – don't use Fire Services UK, they cost a bloody fortune! PR team in there this afternoon, looking for sob stories. I want ten or twelve tearjerkers in tomorrow's papers and some of them on tonight's news.

"Events – I want Oasis 3 or some other dickheads to front a televised gig – all profits to the rescue mission, free samples of heroin to anyone who comes along. And let's think about TV documentaries, let's think about fundraising at public events, in shopping centres, in schools – kids love disasters, don't they? Come on, people, let's get to work and make some cash out of this!"

The Head of PR was frantically scribbling, the two directors were looking at Howard as if they wanted to suck him off. Ewan was also taking notes and had written "Sir Robbie Williams?" on a piece of paper. Surely that old codger couldn't be wheeled out again?

Howard was already striding for the door.

Rosie raised her hand. Ewan tried to push it down again and the commotion caught Howard's eye.

"Yes?" he barked.

"Well – in view of what's happened – shouldn't we take part in the minute's silence this afternoon? We could send a text round to staff?"

"Are you *joking*?" He looked at the others. "Is she *joking*?"

He stared at Rosie as if seeing her for the first time and then looked at Ewan in some disgust.

"I think what Rosie meant to say…" he mumbled.

"I think staff would appreciate it," Rosie interjected.

"Would they now? Would they really? Well, you tell them this. They've got work to do! I didn't sweat my arse off winning that contract so they could stand around moping! Now get to it – and if this gig doesn't come off, you can have as many minutes' silences as you like. Because you won't be working here!"

Rosie felt herself redden as Howard stormed out and slammed the door. Ewan shook his head at her. "I think you put your do-gooder head on for real there," he whispered. "What were you thinking of?"

"Dead people," Rosie said.

19. The perfect job

"Reight. Sit down, Shawn. We need to talk."

Ominous words indeed. Did Keith know I'd come to work with a hangover? Was that against some ancient serial killer's code of conduct?

It had been a hell of a night. Rosie turning up, bottle of wine in her hand, mascara streaking her cheeks. The story of her latest break up. The long chat, the long hugs. The three more bottles of wine.

Then, as she was about to go, the Kiss.

I just kept trying to tell myself I was reading too much into it. Rosie had stood in the doorway, shivering slightly, for ten minutes. Then she smiled at me with a warmth I'd never seen before.

"You are so, so good to me, Sean," she slurred. "I really don't know what I'd do without you."

Swaying on the threshold, I smiled. "You're worth it."

Then, without another word, she'd leaned up and kissed me. On the lips. And it lingered, that kiss. It wasn't purely platonic. It was all I could do not to sling the old tongue in and throw my arms around her. I resisted. The kiss ended.

The kiss ended, but the whirling hadn't yet. I'd lain awake most of the night, musing in my pissed state about whether that had been an off guard moment or whether it meant something more. It had been a strange evening. Rosie was drowning her sorrows about her latest break-up whilst I was secretly celebrating her new single status. We both felt like drinking lots of wine. And after drinking lots of wine, she'd felt like kissing me.

Was it just a spur of the moment thing? Was it just a friendly kiss from the girl next door? Had it just lingered because she was pissed and I'd wanted it to? I couldn't get it out of my mind. The taste of her lip gloss, mingled with the red wine, the softness of her lips against mine. The way that she'd leaned against me, her breasts brushing gently against my chest. God, I was going to remember that moment forever – especially as it might never happen again.

And now the lack of sleep, the bottles of wine and my confused emotional state were forming a deadly combination. I had a searing headache and a dizzy tummy. I sat down facing Keith. I was sweating and nauseous and I must have stunk of booze.

Keith looked at me for a moment. "You alright, Lad?"

"Yeah. Just a bit – tired?"

He nodded. "Reighto. To bisniss."

It was a struggle to concentrate. Keith was talking about some new job that had come in. A "new departure" for the business. I was struggling a bit to make sense of it, because he was talking about morals, and Keith didn't do morals.

"Anyway. I've decided to take on the new line o' work. An' I think it could be the perfect job for you. Break you in nice an' easy."

My ears pricked up at last. Keith had been promising to find me an easy job to launch my career as a murderer. I'd kept hoping he wouldn't find one.

"First thing I should tell you is – yer not goin' to kill anyone. Not yet. Well – not a person, any road up."

I felt hot and confused. "What?"

"Nah. That's the new line. The perfect job. It's a *pet* killin'! Yer goin' to murder a fookin' *moggie*!" And his big body shook with laughter.

"I'm going to – what?"

"It's a fookin' cat! Some lover's revenge thing! I wouldn't normally touch it, but it's reight up yer street!"

"Er – not sure about that – I mean, is killing cats legal?"

"No law 'gainst it. There's a couple a pest control companies specialise in bumpin' off mogs that shit in yer garden. Just not normally my thing. I mean - I *like* animals!"

The sweat was gathering on my forehead and around the back of my neck. "I don't understand, Keith! How am I meant to kill a cat?"

He tried the smiling. "Well, there's more 'n' one way, as they say!"

I looked at him and he did the attempted smiling thing again.

"It's the perfect job for ya. Reight up yer street, Shawn!"

"I'm really not sure it is…"

"Serious, Lad. It is. Some fookin' lesbo, been ditched by 'er bird. All you 'ave to do is rustle the moggie, chop off its 'ead and leave it on 'er doorstep. An' the *easy* part is – it's right up yer street!"

"You keep saying that, but…"

"Well, it is! The lass wi' the cat – Row-sie, they call 'er. An' she lives on yer street!"

Oh fucking, *fucking* hell.

20. The meeting

The secretary's skirt was so short that he could see her black lacy knickers. Lee Macken stifled the urge to give her backside a huge spank as he followed her down the corridor. The cause of Men's Lib hadn't gone quite far enough yet for him to get away with it. Political correctness was on the run, but it probably still had a foothold in the NHS.

The babe turned and smiled. "Is this your first visit to the Millennium Dome, Mr Macken?"

Lee nodded. "I've not had much to do with the Health Service, to be honest."

She smiled again. Hey, he might be in here.

"Impressed?"

He looked downwards. "Who couldn't be?"

There was no question about it, the NHS HQ was deeply impressive. Ok, the look was a bit kitschy for his tastes – all that magnolia paint and old Ikea pictures on the walls – but the sheer scale of it was amazing. The NHS was one of the biggest employers in the UK – its sales team alone was bigger than that of most banks. It employed thousands of accountants, PR people, researchers, security staff, and a fair few doctors and nurses.

The National Health Service had been a joke a few years back – its principles were based on the old Soviet Union and it never made a profit. Now, it was a market leader in delivering health information and treatment to the public. It didn't come cheap - Lee himself favoured the less glamorous end of the market - but there was no doubt that NHS customers were pampered like no other. Whether the actual doctors were any better was debatable – Lee had never had any problem with the more basic services provided by Which Doctor UK.

The babe led him through yet another set of double doors, this one marked SALES SECTION 15. She turned right down a short corridor and tapped on the third door on the right. There was a low hum and the door opened. Sitting behind a huge desk in a gargantuan room, holding a remote control for the door, sat a short, spiky- haired man with huge red glasses and a broad smile.

"Yo! Mr Macken, I presume? Sammy Wonder!"

He stepped out from behind the huge desk and extended his arm. The office was so big that it took a few seconds for the two men's outstretched hands to meet.

"Nice to meet you."

"Pleasure is all mine, Mr Macken. Bella, could you fix us two cappuccinos? Unless you'd prefer a drop of speed?"

"Coffee's fine."

Lee sat down on the chair facing Sammy Wonder's desk. Staring at him was a huge framed photograph on the desk. An alsation dog.

"That's the missus!" beamed Sammy. "No, no, no! I'm kidding! Only kidding! That's Jasper, my best friend in the world!"

Bella the babe smiled thinly. "Two capuccinos coming up."

Lee tried to wink at her, but somehow didn't get it quite right. Instead, the whole right side of his face gave a huge twitch. "Sorry. No sleep last night."

"You dirty dog, Mr Macken!" beamed Sammy. Bella left the room.

"Right, let's get down!" said Sammy, sweeping a hand across his desk and dislodging most of his in-tray. This was going to be educational, if nothing else.

Two hours later, Lee Macken walked out of the Millennium Dome. He felt like punching the air. The contract he'd just signed could set him up for life. It all made sense now. Sammy fucking Wonder had made perfect, life-changing sense.

The NHS, he'd told him, was losing business hand over fist because so many people were opting for murdering those who'd annoyed them, rather than just organising a good kicking, which the NHS could then repair. As a healthcare business, they weren't allowed to run campaigns to get people to opt for less 'final' options and let the good old NHS put the victims together again later.

The Enterprise Act had a clause forbidding the promotion of 'feeder' businesses by both policing and healthcare businesses. And this crazy bit of red tape was about to make Lee Macken rich.

"We want to go into partnership with a punishment beating provider. We'll give you the dosh, secure the staff you need – and to run a funky PR campaign about the value of a good hiding. We're talking wall to wall ad space – everything from BBC Sky to the Microsoft Channels. You are that partner, buddy boy. You hear me, Mr Macken? Welcome to the family!"

Then they'd talked figures. Sammy Wonder may have looked and talked like an idiot, but Macken could have snogged the little freak. He'd just offered a partnership which would give him advertising and staffing resources beyond his wildest dreams. If he started taking business off murderers, he'd really be on the map. It even fitted in, if you thought about it, with his beloved strapline – *Protecting the Community*. Oh yeah – I'll protect them alright! Protect them from something much worse – a date with Keith Hartley or someone like him. Another slogan was already forming in his mind – *Don't let them off the hook - make the bastards suffer*.

Suddenly, the sky was the limit for GBH Unlimited.

21. The refugee

I did not want to find Sara on the doorstep today. I truly did not. Had I listened to the news instead of going through the day in a daze following my meeting with Keith, I'd've been relieved. But I'd missed the fact that there'd been another environmental disaster and that it had happened in my home town. So it was with a sigh of disbelief that I greeted her. She wasn't best pleased.

"Some welcome that. You should be glad I'm alive."

Her opening gambit did not alert me to the nature of the tragedy she'd survived. My little sister uses that kind of terminology all the time. Her life is a series of 'disasters' and apparently life-threatening arguments with boyfriends, neighbours, employers and police companies. The combination of her tempestuous nature and her extreme radical views means she is rarely out of trouble – and her travails are rarely assisted by any sense of perspective.

She's annoyingly pretty – long dark hair, big hazel eyes, model figure – and maybe this has contributed to her being such a prima donna. As she glowered at me, I got that feeling a million boyfriends, neighbours, employers and police officers must have had before me – that I was about to come under attack. But then when I looked closely, I could see tears forming. This was all I fucking needed today.

But when she told me what had happened, it came as more of a shock that I'd expected. The old place in Eastbourne demolished. Shitting hell, what a day. My old life and my new life being destroyed at the same time. How the fuck had I missed hearing about this on the news? Why hadn't my dad called me from Spain? Oh shit, he had – three or four times. I just hadn't fancied an update on the day to day lives of the ultra-dull expats my parents now shared their lives with. Not today, anyway.

"I knew yesterday, " Sara sobbed. "It was so scary. The tide just kept coming nearer and nearer. The rain pissing down all day and night. And it was so *dark*! I kept waiting for you to phone! Where the fuck have you *been*!"

I put my arms around her now. "I'm really sorry," I gulped. "I've not been paying much attention to anything recently."

"Not even to your sister *drowning*?"

"I didn't know," I said. "I'm really sorry. I didn't know."

Sara had elected to stay on in Eastbourne when my parents headed for Spain a few years ago, after the last floods had wiped out the entire sea front. House prices were dirt cheap by the sea now and Mum and Dad had agreed eventually to sell up to her. I knew they'd always worried about her living at the seaside – my dad used to say it reminded him of his father smoking – "You're basically electing to kill yourself." But the changing demographic of seaside towns appealed to Sara. Full of young people, parties and hedonistic attitudes. Now, Eastbourne was just full of sea.

"I can't find Greg and I can't find Melissa. I haven't seen either of them since yesterday and they're not answering their phones! I'm really scared they're dead, Sean. Melissa loved watching storms and I can just imagine…"

"Try not to imagine anything. I'm sure there's all sorts of problems getting hold of people right now," I said, resuming my oft-played role of sympathetic older brother, while wondering again how on earth I'd missed all this. And thinking that Greg and Melissa were almost certainly goners.

So instead of planning the murder of the pussycat next door, I spent the evening comforting Sara, speaking to my parents from Spain and feeling like it was the worst day of my life. Mum and Dad reacted exactly as I thought they would. Dad started complaining about how irresponsible the Government was and the last million or so governments before it. It was clearly their fault and not Sara's for living in a town where you couldn't get insurance because scientists had been predicting for years with absolute certainty that it would end up in the sea. And, of course, my parents' decision to sell the house to the spoilt brat for the price of a bottle of sun lotion was equally irrelevant.

"Government after government has let us down. All of us." It doesn't take much to get my Dad on this subject, how communities have collapsed, how standards have declined and everything's going to the dogs. Even the press. My Dad was proud of his stint on the now afloat Eastbourne Times and the standards of fine journalism he'd been responsible for. Not the same now, of course, with the papers generally owned by the likes of Whores4U and Porn U Like.

My Mum, of course, found the whole thing a little bit hilarious. My Mum has always had the philosophy that there is a funny side to everything. It's almost the polar opposite to my Dad's view that there's a serious side to most things and it's usually the government's fault. I don't know quite how they rub along together so well. My Mum spent a full two minutes laughing hysterically about a picture she'd seen in the news of a dog swimming in circles around the rubble that had been its house. It takes a special sense of humour to do that.

Sara played my parents with frankly admirable style and theatricality: a cheque was put in the post, which I hoped meant she wouldn't stay long. Both Sara and my parents were assuming she'd be staying here and I'd no choice but to agree – there is no spare bed, meaning I would have the sofa, at least until the cheque arrives.

My flat is quite unusual in layout. Like lots of London flats, it's basically part of a converted house - I don't have my own front door, I share that with Rosie, which is a nice thought. You walk in to my half of the building from the hallway and you're in the living room, which leads through to the kitchen and then the bedroom and then the bathroom. It's essentially a long sequence of rooms and all the flats are the same – Rosie's, which is across the hall from mine, has the same peculiar setup. But what mine has that her doesn't is a cellar underneath the kitchen. You basically open what looks like a kitchen cupboard and nearly fall down a steep, narrow flight of stairs. It covers the whole area of the flat, so it is theoretically a great area for another bedroom or living area, but I largely use it as a dumping ground. It's also cold, dark and gloomy and once you've tired of surprising drunken friends by asking them to open the door, not very interesting. But maybe it was about to fulfil its potential and become a somewhat depressing bedroom.

So all in all, the task Keith had presented me with wasn't getting any easier. Sara is a bit of a hippy type and probably very anti-murder – especially in the case of cats. Maybe I'd have to put the killing on hold a while. Keith wouldn't like that – and today, for the first time, I got the sense that he was demanding I step up to the plate. I wasn't sure quite what would happen if I refused to take the job on and I didn't really want to think about it. The man was a notorious psychopath. It was hard to imagine him just giving me my cards. And I couldn't bear the thought of fleeing with Rosie's kiss still so fresh in my mind.

No, I had little alternative but to perform the vile task he'd given me. That fucking bitch Shirley – I always knew she was off her face. She'd be fucking delighted if she knew how things had turned out. Every time it came into my mind, my soul shuddered. I felt like I'd rather kill myself than Rosie's cat. Maybe that was the answer…

"Are you ok?"

Sara was looking at me.

"Just tired. A bit shocked, you know."

"It's just you keep drifting off. Staring into the distance. I mean, I'm sorry if my near death is boring you!"

"It's not that. Not at all. Just a bit shaken up."

"*You're* shaken up! Walk a mile in my shoes!"

I'd love to, I thought. There's nothing I'd love more than to walk a mile in *anyone* else's shoes right now. Yeah, Sara's house was in the sea, her friends probably were too. But she didn't have to plot the murder of the beloved pet of the person she was in love with. Either that, or face the wrath of Britain's most notorious murderer. Little did she know it, but my sister had it easy.

22. Question time

A huge jeer went up as Betsy Saunders rose to her feet in the Kellogs House of Commons. Everyone remembered what had happened the last time she'd intervened on the floor of the House and the Coalitionists were hoping for more of the same. Gregory Styles had just bombarded the Prime Minister with a series of questions about the Eastbourne disaster, saying that the Government had a duty to intervene rather than leaving everything to British American Heroin, who were running the rescue mission. The PM – a foppish ex-journalist called Horace Ronson – was typically dismissive, accusing Styles of advocating communism.

"You talk about modernising your party and then you come up with suggestions that an old Marxist like Ted Heath would have been proud of! Once again, what we get from you is . . . all *Styles* and no *substance*!"

The Coalition benches loved that, and their mood of jubilation increased as Britain's Most Left Wing MP rose to her feet.

"Where's your earpod?" one shouted. Betsy had to steady herself. The urge to shout 'Go fuck yourself' was strong, but she knew it wouldn't help her cause.

"Mr Speaker," she said. "Given the tragic events of this week, I hope you will forgive me for raising another matter."

The Government benches cheered wildly. "Enterprise Act!" they chorused.

Betsy paused and went on. "I wish to raise the matter of a constituent of mine who has been dismissed from her job as a prostitute, following her reporting an unlicensed assault."

The Coalitionists jeered again and Betsy ignored the sighs and tongue-clicking on her own side. Whores weren't a vote winner. They all knew that.

"The company refused to report the unlicensed assault, because it was carried out, I'm afraid to say – by a member of the Government."

There was a stunned silence. Then uproar.

Members on both sides of the House shouted at their opposite numbers – the Coalitionists in blind panic, the People's Party with glee. The Coalitionists were demanding that she sit down.

"Order!" yelled the Speaker, "Order! The Honourable Lady cannot make such a…"

Betsy shouted above him. "Given his supposed commitment to *Decent Values*, will the Prime Minister promise the House a full investigation into this matter?" She had to shout louder. "And will he promise to sack any member of his Government who…"

"The Honourable Member must withdraw!" bellowed the Speaker. "She must withdraw unless she can substantiate such serious allegations about an honourable member!"

Betsy looked at the bench opposite her and to her delight saw Richard Splash scowling in quivering discomfort.

"Mr Speaker, I can and I will substantiate what I'm saying! I can name here and now which *Cabinet minister…*"

Now the uproar reached a crescendo. MPs on both sides of the House were on their feet, shouting at each other.

"Order! Order! *Order!*" shrieked the Speaker, but he was getting nowhere. Betsy too was unable to make herself heard over the deafening row. Splash was one of those MPs on his feet, gesticulating wildly. Their eyes met and he gave her a look of pure venom. All around them, MPs were yelling at the tops of their voices and almost coming to blows. The Sarge At Arms Ltd team were standing in between three or four of the more vociferous members.

Eventually, as the din started to subside, the Speaker raised his hand. "This sitting of the House is hereby suspended!" he announced. "We shall reconvene tomorrow, when members have had the chance to collect themselves and to behave with some decorum!"

But Betsy wasn't finished. As the MPs filed out, she saw one of the TV cameras zooming in on her.
"I was talking," she shouted angrily. "About

the Minister for Free Enterprise - Mr Richard Splash!"

A new commotion kicked off now, with Splash screaming angrily that she was a liar and the Speaker demanding that she leave the House immediately. The Sarge at Arms Limited team were indeed limited – most of them were former dinner ladies from Darlington, but at least they had come cheap. Now there was fighting on the floor of the House and Splash was shrieking that he was going to sue. Behind her, Betsy felt Ryan's hand on her arm, pushing her towards the exit. She didn't struggle as the oil man ushered her away.

23. Revenge

Sadie shivered as she walked up the steps of the Mircrosoft Corporation. She'd never been on television before and this was a big ordeal. But it meant Revenge and that was all that mattered.

The receptionist gave a cold smile when Sadie gave her name. That name had been in every national newspaper today and she was now the most famous whore in Britain – ironic, really for someone who wasn't technically a whore anymore – though on that front, offers were already flooding in. All the competitors trying to make Whores 4 U look like bastards. Blow Girls had seemed especially interested in the fact that she'd lost her front teeth.

A florid looking young man in an expensive suit had appeared by her side.

"Sadie Lister? I'm Martin Miles. Associate producer." He shook her hand vigorously. "So pleased you could come in. Would you like a coffee?"

"Do you have coke?" Sadie asked.

"Sure. There's a vending machine in the canteen. Coke, hash, speed, whatever you fancy."

Sadie followed him to the canteen, where he insisted on paying for her line. As she snorted, he babbled. It seemed Richard Splash was threatening to sue Betsy Saunders and anyone else who repeated the allegations she had made. The corporation was nervous and Martin Miles' head was on the block.

"I s'pose what I'm saying is, it would be great if you had some sort of documentary proof. Apart from the teeth thingy, that is. Our Mr Splash is a very powerful person."

"You think I don't know that? Bastard cost me my job."

"Of course. Sorry. But the thing is – it's still your word against his. Your old bosses are playing hardball, refusing to confirm that he was a customer. It puts the corporation on a bit of a sticky wicket, you get me?"

"It's up to you. I can always go home if you don't want the interview."

His face fell. "Oh, but we do, we do. We really do. I just sort of hoped that – well, I guess it was a long shot. But you know Jeremy will be quite tough with you?"

"Jeremy?"

"Our interviewer. He has to be seen to – well, sort of interrogate you. You've made quite serious allegations against a Cabinet minister, you know."

"I know. They're true."

"I don't doubt that, but…"

"Well neither should Jeremy or anyone else, then. If he wants to have a go at me, he'll get it back."

He smiled. "Well, as long as you know what to expect. Even if he doesn't!" And he laughed, rather too much, and snorted what was left of her coke.

After the coke break, he led her into the studio – a huge room, with blazing lights and lots of people running around. In the middle of the studio was a large table, where a very tall, greying man with a snooty expression sat leafing through a porn magazine. Martin Miles led Sadie across to him.

"Hi Jez, this is Sadie. The whore."

'Jez' waved his arm at the chair on the other side of the table. He didn't look up and continued to read his porn mag. Sadie sat there in silence for what seemed like hours, but was probably a couple of minutes. She was too hot. But the coke had kicked in and she was feeling confident. Mr Porno could have a go at her if he wanted. She had right on her side.

Eventually, Martin shouted. "Ok, people five seconds . . five, four, three, two, one – go, Jeremy!"

The porn mag was discarded on the floor and Jeremy suddenly looked elegant and distinguished as he stared at a camera that had just zoomed in on them.

"Well, I'm joined now by Sadie Lister, the prostitute at the centre of what's being called the

Splashgate affair. Miss Lister – you've made some very serious charges against a member of the Cabinet. Can you prove them?"

Sadie smiled gappily. "Well, before I met Mr Splash, I had a full set of teeth."

"Yes, well that's not exactly proof, is it?"

Sadie shrugged. "It's all the proof I got, Love."

Jeremy frowned slightly. "And yet your former employer, Whores 4 U, has refused to back up your story. And they've said that you were dismissed because you were – and I quote – unreliable. So why should we believe you?"

"Look, Honey, I don't really care whether you believe me or not. And I'll tell you how reliable I was. I spent 16 hours a day on my back for that lot. First sign of trouble, I was given the shove."

Jeremy looked taken aback, but pressed on.

"Why didn't you report the matter to one of the police companies?"

"'Cos I'm not made of money. I reported the matter to my MP instead."

"Yes, you did. To Betsy Saunders - hardly the most reputable of MPs. She took you at face value and she then made allegations under parliamentary privilege about an opponent she is known to detest. As a result, a respected minister is fighting to save his job. But we still have no proof. Just – frankly -

the word of a whore against that of a Cabinet minister."

"An ex-whore, actually."

"Yes, well. Maybe soon we'll be talking about an ex-Cabinet minister…"

"Let's hope so."

Jeremy looked irritated now and fiddled with his earpiece.

"So let's get this straight. You're very happy to see a man once tipped as a future Prime Minister lose his job over allegations you have made?"

"I'd be thrilled to bits, Love. The man's a complete tosser. And I'll tell you something else. He's got a black mole on his scrotum. Right above his bollocks."

She could hear sharp intakes of breath all over the studio. Jeremy was stunned into silence.

"Now tell me, *Jez*," she said. "How would a lying whore like me know that?"

She'd wiped the floor with the cocky bastard, she thought, as she sat in the canteen afterwards doing another line. The studio phones had gone into meltdown. Martin Miles had been on his mobile ever since. Jeremy had looked grey and stunned as he drew the interview to a close. Already, bids were being made to get Richard Splash to come on TV and deny that he had a mole on his scrotum. "Minister brought down by a whore and a mole," she heard someone say in the canteen. "It's like the good old days!"

Sadie walked down the steps of the Microsoft Corporation and stood looking down the street, smiling to herself. Revenge was very sweet. A car had pulled up in front of her – not paparazzi again, for fuck's sake. No. A black man in a baseball cap had jumped out of the car, holding a machine gun. A hitman. It didn't even occur to Sadie that she was the hit.

24. The survivors

Rosie had just got off to sleep when she was awakened by a piercing scream. What the hell was that? She rolled over and looked at her bedside remote. 11.40. Some sort of commotion going on outside. Next door? Sean! Fuck, she'd never contacted him to ask about his sister! And there was a right hysterical racket going on there now.

She jumped out of bed and pulled on her jeans over her nightshirt. There was a man laughing, someone else sobbing now. She picked up the remote that switched on the light, then ran out in to her living room. Another press on the remote opened her front door. Sean's door across the hall was wide open and that was where the racket was coming from.

Rosie walked in to Sean's place through the open door. Two girls in the centre of the room were leaping up and down, hugging and screaming. A cute bloke with dreadlocks was standing behind them, smiling. And Sean was sitting on the sofa in his boxers, his hair tousled, rubbing his eyes and looking bemused.

One of the girls broke free from the melee in the middle of the room and ran towards Rosie, arms outstretched. Rosie recognised her – it was Sean's sister.

"ROSIE!" she yelled. "Yeah!! Listen, this is fantastic! I want you to meet . . . this is my friend Greg, and my friend Melissa. They got caught in a tidal wave at Eastbourne. And they're *alive*!!! I can't believe it! Do you remember me? Sara! Sean's sister. They're *alive*! Oh, my *God*!"

Rosie nodded and smiled at Sara's friends. Both looked a bit like people who'd had a rough couple of days. Greg's T-shirt and jeans were torn, though that may of course be a fashion statement. Melissa – a small black woman with spiky hair and an engaging grin – looked like she'd been pulled from the sea only minutes ago. She looked soaked and frozen – but she was smiling from ear to ear.

Sean gave Rosie a 'how did you get here' look. He looked funny sitting there in his underwear. She had a vague recollection that she'd nearly snogged him the other night. Not a good idea.

Sara was jumping up and down again. "Sean – this calls for a celebration! Can we order a takeaway? They're *alive*!"

Sean looked from one person to the other in his living room. Then slowly, he smiled. He never had a good word to say for his little sister, but Rosie knew he actually loved her dearly.

"Yeah," he said. "Fuck work in the morning! There's a number in my phone, Rosie – they're called All Night Long. Get coke, Es, champers, beers – anything you want. Stick it on my account."

He looked at Rosie, as if seeking her approval.

"I don't mind," she said, confused.

"Well I hope you don't, cos you're invited!" shrieked Sara, who was spinning round the room again.

"Ah, work in the morning …" began Rosie, but Melissa cut her off.

"You heard the man! *Fuck* work in the morning! Come on!"

Sara took picked up her earpod from the coffee table and plugged it into the giant speaker in the corner. Oasis 3 burst into *Live Forever* at 400 decibels and she and Melissa started to dance around the now vibrating room. Sean sat there in his boxers, not giving a shit and beaming at Rosie.

"Can I just go home and get changed?" she tried to shout over the din, but Melissa had already grabbed her and pulled her on to the makeshift dancefloor.

25. The party

Greg is a bit of an activist. Correction, he is not active at all. He has never worked a day in his life. But he calls himself an activist because he goes on lots of 'demonstrations', like some 20th century throwback. The demos seem to consist of chanting slogans while throwing stones at whoever is doing security, but Greg assures me he and his comrades are making the world a better place.

"Man, we gotta get rid of the corporates. We gotta get rid of the rich. Smash everything up and start again," he droned. "You know what? A hundred years ago, we were free. *Unchained*, man! All we had to protest about was fast food and wars about oil. And when people said that the planet was headed for oblivion, the politicians laughed. But the planet is fighting back, man. Today Eastbourne, tomorrow the rest of the UK. We better grow some gills, man."

Or alternatively, grow some weed and ruin parties by talking bollocks.

"Well," I said. "There's a lot of the top companies working on the climate. I think we'll have an answer one day soon."

Greg snorted and Sara and Melissa laughed. "Are you for real, man? *Corporates* tryin' to save the world? Why'd they wanna do that?" He looked genuinely amazed.

"Er – dunno, Greg. Maybe 'cos they live here too?"

Rosie chuckled, but the others looked at me in varying degrees of rage for daring to be sarky to the mighty guru.

"You wanna make fun of it, that's cool, man. But we nearly died today. And the people who pulled us out of the flood weren't corporates. They were activists."

"Actually," Rosie interjected, rather unwisely, "They *were* corporates. They were employed by British American Heroin. I know because I work there. We ran the whole operation."

Greg was staring a long, stoned hard stare as Sara squealed at Rosie.

"You work for those *bastards*! Rosie, how could you! They're murdering *scum*!"

Rosie smiled a bit too patronisingly. "Not today, they're not. They've saved thousands of lives. Including your friends' here."

"That's where you're wrong, actually," Melissa said, her smile gone. "The lads who pulled us out were activists, not smack pushers!"

"The lads who pulled you out were part of VSU – Voluntary Services Underseas. They were employed by us and had exclusive rights to the rescue mission. There were no hippies allowed – it just so happens that some of them dress a bit like you."

Oh shit, I shouldn't have ordered all that coke and booze.

"That is scandalous!" Greg whined. "Scandalous! Exclusive rights to a rescue mission! You could have saved hundreds more if you'd just let guys help out, man. People dying so your company can have their name in lights. Sick, man!"

Melissa was on her feet now. "You know what? They should have fucking drowned us! Cos they're killing us all anyway! They should have let us fucking *drown*!"

Rosie smirked. "Well, I'm not arguing with that." Fucking hell, what had got in to her tonight?

Now Sara was on her feet too. "You take that back! You take that back or get out! I can't believe you said that!"

Greg raised his hand. "It's cool. She works for the corporates. They want us to die because we're exposing the truth about them. If they'd known who we were…"

Rosie laughed out loud. "Oh yeah, they're really terrified of you guys! Your picture is plastered all over our intranet! You're our most wanted man!"

Melissa's eyes had widened. "Really? Shit, Greg…" And now her wide eyes shone at him.

"No, not really," said Rosie, laughing again. "Jesus Christ, if saving the planet is up to you guys, we're may as well all go to Eastbourne and jump in!"

Melissa scowled. Greg scowled. Sara stormed out of the room and slammed the door.

"What a swell party this is," I said. "Thanks for dropping in, guys."

Rosie was clearly enjoying it all a bit too much. "Hey Sean!" she slurred. "Tell the activists what your job is!"

I smiled. "Nah. They've had a tough time and I think it's time we called a truce."

"No really, please tell us!" spat Melissa. "What are you? A butcher? A police officer? It can't be any worse than what she does! Murderer!"

The self-righteousness was the clincher. "Actually, yes."

Melissa put on an annoyingly accurate imitation of my voice. "'*Actually yes*' what?"

"Actually, yes, I'm a murderer. That's my job. I work for Keith Hartley."

They both stared at me. I nodded benignly. They stared back. Rosie covered her mouth, stifling another outburst of laughter.

Eventually, Greg rose to his feet.

"Man, you are a fucking disgrace. A fucking *disgrace*! Well, I will not suck the cock of a killer, whoever's bro she is."

"Oh, you don't need to do that, " I said. "Just snort all the coke and drink all the booze that I paid for by killing people."

"No, man. I won't do it."

"You already did it, Bozo."

Greg strode across the room, his eyes blazing. "Listen, man, I'm not a violent man…"

I stood up and towered over him. Fuck, he was a shortarse.

"I am, though," I said.

Greg lowered his head and smiled shruggily.

"Yeah. Well I won't take tea with no murderer!"

And he strode out. Melissa glared at us both, spat on the floor and then followed him.

I went to the door after them and shouted down the street. "What's all this taking tea and sucking cocks? Why not just freeload off me then storm off when you're losing the argument? You CUNTS!"

Rosie was laughing her head off, but now Sara had appeared behind me. "What the fuck's going on? Where are Greg and Melissa?"

"Off to start the fucking revolution!" I said. "This time tomorrow, Greg will be Prime Minister!"

Rosie guffawed again.

"You're such a fucking cock, Sean." Sara said and headed off to the bathroom. More slamming. Then I could hear her on her mobile, apologising profusely to the radicals as they stormed parliament or slept on a park bench or whatever they were doing now.

Rosie was laughing herself silly. Stoned, pissed, floating silly. "That was fantastic!" she said. "It's really cheered me up!"

I grinned at her. "Knobheads," I said.

Then she stood up, put her arms around my neck and kissed me passionately.

What a swell party this was.

26. The morning after

There's something gnawing at my soul. Something that won't go away.

For some reason, my Mum is laughing her head off, but there's a hippy bloke with a dog swimming around and around my old house in Eastbourne. I can't see Sara or Dad anywhere. The hippy is shouting something about corporate liars and a girl in a T-shirt with a giant needle on it is sailing past in a boat, laughing merrily. Mum can't stop laughing and now the dog has disappeared under the water. The hippy bloke is thrashing around, swearing. I think his name is Greg. *I can't see Dad or Sara anywhere.* Are they dead?

The girl in the boat is naked. She's not laughing anymore. She's smiling at me, seductively, but I can't concentrate. I can't concentrate on Dad and Sara, because Rosie is naked. *The poor old dog was drowned.* But *you and I, we're going to live forever.*

I need to pee, really desperately need to pee. My throat burns, my eyes ache, I need to pee. But I'm rock hard. How can I pee when I'm rock hard? There's a song on the radio. It's Duran Duran 4, singing *Don't say a prayer for me now, save it till the morning after.* There's someone waffling about Eastbourne and dedicating the song to all those who died and I don't know where Sara is. Dad's in Spain, I remember now. Mum is laughing her arse off. Rosie is naked, stark naked, and she's curled up next to me. In her bed. My head hurts. I really, really need to pee now.

Fuck, I'm not dreaming. *I'm not dreaming*!

I was, but now I'm not. *This bit was not a dream.*

Rosie is lying next to me, naked.

I remember . . . everything. Rosie writhing in my arms, my lips on her skin, all over her body, her mouth and hands everywhere, her moans, her taste, her perfume and the way it mingled with our sweat, the sheer thrill of our tongues entwining as we made love, I can still feel everything. How many times? Fucking Es are magic. How many times? At least four. Ok, I really, really need to pee now.

I untangled myself from Rosie's legs and stumbled out of her bed, still proudly erect. What the *fuck*? Sara was standing in the doorway.

"Oops," she said. "Sorr-ee!" And she stood there and folded her arms.

That did the trick - I'd have no problem pissing now. I brushed her out of the way and headed into Rosie's bathroom. What the fuck was Sara doing in Rosie's flat?

"Oy! Do you remember what an arse you were last night?" she shouted through the door after me. "Well, I've just come to say that I'm leaving!"

The pee was absolute ecstasy, but it went on and on and on and on and on. Eventually, the power of speech trickled back, though it hurt my body and soul. "Don't go," I croaked. "Let's talk about it."

No answer. I opened the bathroom door and Sara was gone. I ran to the front door, then realised I was naked. I ran to the living room window. No sign. Ah, fuck it. I felt too rough today to deal with all this. Back to bed. Back to bed with Rosie. Fucking hell. I felt shit shit shit, but I felt like I'd won a squillion quid.

I turned around to find her standing there. Starkers. Christ, her body was to die for. Firm, slightly plump breasts, dark brown nipples, gorgeous round shoulders. curved tummy, good legs, even cute feet. There was nothing wrong with her body at all. Nothing. I smiled cheesily.

She shook her head while rubbing her eyes. "Big mistake, huh?" she said, and wandered back in to her bedroom.

Now, hang on. Hang on a fucking *minute*. Something's gone wrong with the script here.

27. The morning after, part II

"You mean the party? Rosie?"

Oh, poor Sean. Rosie covered her eyes with her hand and pulled the sheet tighter around her.

"I meant us. You know I did."

Sean stood in the doorway, looking suddenly vulnerable in his nakedness. He ran his hands through his hair, then suddenly bent down and fished his boxers out of the pile of clothes on the floor and staggered into them gracelessly. Then he sat down on the end of her bed.

How the fuck could she have been so stupid? She'd known how he felt. She'd known all along. What on earth had possessed her to end up in bed with him? 'Ending up in bed'. When people said that, Rosie usually laughed. How do you 'end up' having sex someone by accident? Surely there has to be a bit of premeditation, a hint of desire, somewhere along the line?

There had certainly been no shortage of desire when they'd got down to it last night. She could feel herself flushing as she remembered it. He may have an ordinary face and an ordinary body and an ordinary – well, everything - but that had been a fabulous shag. Or shags. Fuck, how many times had they done it? All those things he'd done to her – all the things she'd done in return. Fuck, it had been good – dirty, desperate, delightful. She still felt the first two of those, but a long way from the third. Last night was another world now.

"You're joking, right?" he said after a long pause.

"I'm sorry. It was nice. It was – great. But you and me – we're not about that."

"Not about what? What do you mean?"

"Not about sex. We're - well, we're friends, aren't we?"

He was shaking his head now. "I don't get this, Rosie."

She sat up and put a hand on his arm. "Nor do I, mate. I'm sorry."

They sat like that for some time. She was scared he was going to cry. Then Timmy wandered in demanding his breakfast, and Sean jumped slightly.

"Fuck! What's the time?"

She looked at the remote. "Half eleven."

"Fuck! Keith'll kill me!"

He leapt up and tried to tug his jeans on, but Timmy was rubbing around his legs and he tripped over the cat, going sprawling across the floor. He lay there for a moment, then tried to get up, but seemed to think better of it. There he lay in the middle of her room, jeans on one leg, facing up to the ceiling, and sighed.

There was an ache in that sigh that was tangible.

Rosie felt sick. She also felt an overwhelming warmth towards her fallen friend. He looked so defeated, so awkward, his hopes like his jeans waving around his ankles, as Timmy sniffed at his face in what looked like mock sympathy.

She lay back on the bed. "Oh fuck it, Sean," she said. "Just come back to bed."

"What?"

"Just come back to bed with me."

He thrashed about the floor a bit, fell over a couple of times, but basically didn't need asking twice.

28. Job satisfaction

Richard Splash was absolutely mortified. To think that he, a Cabinet minister – the rising star of the Coalition benches and, whisper it quietly, many people's favourite to be the next Prime Minister – should be sitting in a police station being questioned about an illegal murder. All the achievements, the radical reforms he and others had strived for, sacrificed on the altar of political correctness. PC was not dead after all – why else would this nonsense of not allowing politicians to commission murders persist? And he'd known that *Decent Values* campaign was a bollocks idea.

Nick Rankin, on the other hand, was enjoying himself. Police UK was a dull place to work most of the time. The older officers still ranted on about the old days, when the nanny state police force had sweeping powers and virtually everything was a criminal offence You could drive around arresting shoplifters in the morning, investigate a murder or two in the afternoon and catch burglars red-handed at night. Although some of the cynics said that that rarely happened – that in reality they'd spent most of their time filling out forms and mouthing platitudes to homeowners who had been burgled as the stable door swung gaily behind them - it stood to reason that policing would be fun if more things were actually illegal.

But questioning a Cabinet Minister – this was the stuff of police dreams! He'd seen this little shit on the telly now and then, and hated him on sight. Arrogant, self-important, ugly little toad. He had little doubt that Splash had been involved in the whore's killing somewhere along the line, but he knew proving it would be difficult. That wouldn't stop him giving the prick a hard time and taking him down a peg or two.

"So you categorically deny any involvement whatsoever in Miss Lister's murder?"

"Of course I do. I'm an MP and MPs aren't allowed to kill people. End of."

"They're not, are they, sir? And you know that includes arranging and commissioning killings?"

"I'm the bloody Minister for Free Enterprise, you clown! Do you think I don't know my own laws?"

Rankin bristled. "I'd thank you not to take that tone with me, Mr Splash. You are facing a very serious charge here."

"Oh, am I now? Am I weally? Face it, you've not a scwap of evidence to go on! Not a scwap! You've hauled me in here, away fwom important parliamentawy business, on the basis of a scuwilous allegation fwom the cwaziest MP in the countwy! And there just happens to be a vanload of pappawazzi waiting outside to film the whole thing! Well let me tell you this, Wankin – I'll be suing Police UK over this!"

"What did you call me, sir?"

"Wankin! It's your name, is it not?"

"No. Rankin. With an R."

"That's what I said. Wankin."

"Blimey! You want to run the country and you can't even speak properly! I'm in the wrong job!"

"You most certainly are, Mr Wankin – but west assured, you won't be in it much longer! Taking that tone with a Minister of the Cwown! It's outwageous!"

Splash's reddened face was a picture. Christ, this was fun.

"Well, I can let you have a complaint form before you leave, sir – assuming you can write ok – sorry…" Rankin rolled the 'r' with a grin. "Wrrrrite ok?"

Splash was on his feet. "How dare you! I will not spoken to like this!'"

"Sit down!" barked Rankin, so fiercely that Splash obeyed meekly. "Now, listen to me. I'm going to get to the bottom of this murky business whether you like it or not. I've asked whether you want a lawyer…"

"I don't need one. These are twumped up charges and you a jumped up fool! Welease me at once!"

"Your choice. All I can do is let you know your whites. Sorry, *rights!* Capital Hitmen have named the person who took out the contract as one Niall Burke. This Burke is being questioned in another room as we speak. I'm about to have the pleasure of meeting him. He hasn't as yet come up with a plausible motive for the murder – and I intend on asking some very searching questions about his ...connections."

"This is an outwage!" choked Splash. "To question a pwivate citizen about why he might choose to have someone killed. This is political cowectness gone mad! I will have no part in this chawade, Wankin!"

"I'm sorry, sir. But you've no choice in the matter. This murder is extremely suspicious in my opinion and I intend to find out if the law has been broken."

"Either charge me or welease me immediately, Wankin!"

Rankin rose to his feet. "I can't, sir. If you want to be released, you'll need to contact your solicitor. And I have to tell you that until I'm satisfied you're not behind all this, I'll be recommending against it."

"This is an outwage!" wailed Splash again. "Call my lawyer at once, Wankin!"

Rankin paused on his way out. "I can't do two things at once. But I'll get on to it," he smirked. "You know, sir, I'm just doing my job."

And for once, enjoying it immensely.

29. The ultimatum

"Where the fook 'ave you been?" Keith glowered at me as I walked sheepishly into the office. "Two fookin' days I've been callin' ya! Well?"

He looked fierce, but it was hard not to break into a smile. The two days he'd been calling me had been the best of my whole life.

"Sorry, Keith," I said. "Something really urgent came up. My sister nearly drowned in that flood at Eastbourne."

"Do I look like I give two shits? You've a job to do 'ere and you've not bin in. You've not called me, you've ignored me callin' you! Why?"

He folded his arms menacingly.

"I'm really sorry. It was a genuine crisis."

"My arse a crisis. She's still alive, in't she? Like 'alf o' the folk we're supposed to ave murdered! Cos I've been sat 'ere on my arse tryin' to gerrold of you!"

"Oh. Has a backlog built up?"

"There's no fookin' backlog. There's no fookin' bisniss! 'Ave you seen all this shite from GBH Unlimited? Fookin' posters everywhere. TV ads day an' night. Where the fook were you? You don't give two shits about this place!"

Christ, Keith was actually upset. More than that, he finally needed me. It seemed GBH had launched some huge advertising campaign, directly targeting Keith's potential customers. He wanted me to think about how we responded. His own tactic to date has been to ring up their MD and threaten to slit his throat, and to demolish every poster he'd come across – including a billboard opposite his shop. It wasn't looking good. Police UK were investigating the death threat as an anti-competitive practice and would be calling this afternoon to interview him.

"The one fookin' time ya might be able to 'elp and you go fookin' AWOL. Fookin' useless twat!"

Did I detect the ghost of an opportunity here?

Worth a try…

"I'm really sorry, Keith. I know I've been crap. And to be honest, I'm prepared to offer my resignation."

"You can stick yer resignation up yer arse, ya mincin' little tosser! I eed yer 'elp. I need to think about cheap an' cheerful advertisin' and I need some press coverage. Soon as! This is a fookin' *crisis* for this place! You need to pull yer weight for once!"

"Ok – should I concentrate on the PR stuff full time? You do the murders, I'll do the PR?"

Keith screwed his face up and looked at me, as if trying to work out where I was coming from. He spoke slowly, his hand running through his thinning hair.

"No. I need ya start fulfillin' yer potential. Showin' the *madness*. Do the girly shit, yeah, but ya need a couple o' mur-ders under yer belt an' all. Don't ya think?"

He carried on scrutinising me.

I smiled. "Ok. Fine by me."

"Is it?"

I looked back at him. "What do you mean?"

He paused. "'Ave you killed that cat yet?"

I could feel my face starting to burn a bit. I'd fed Timmy only this morning.

"Er – no. Haven't seen the little shit for days on end."

Keith shook his head. "Reight. So we're further behind schedule than I thought."

"I'm sorry. I'm sure he'll turn up."

He walked across the shop and put both hands on my shoulders. "This," he said slowly, deliberately. "Is not good enough. Nowhere *near* good enough!"

He pressed down hard on my shoulders and stared into my face. His eyes were boring right through to my skull. I could feel my own eyes filling with tears. Oh f*uck, please don't cry, Sean!*

He carried on, now shaking my shoulders. "You came to me, Shawn! Ya wanted to be a murderer. I've taken ya on, trained ya up – it's time to deliver, Fella!"

"Y-yes…"

He shook me again. "Stop bein' such a fookin' puff! I will take no more excuses! That fookin' pussy dies tonight – and *this* fook:n pussy kills it! Do you 'ear me? I said, *do you 'ear me*?!"

When Keith bellowed, the whole shop shook. To my mortal horror, I let out a bit of a scream. He released me from his grip and walked across the shop, turning to glare at me.

"I'll do it. I'll track him down and … do it. Tonight."

He folded his arms in clear suspicion.

"I promise, Keith."

"Reight. 'Ere's the deal. The cat dies tonight, you keep ya job. The cat lives – you don't."

Sounded fair. Sounded *good*, actually. I nodded.

He looked at me curiously.

"Ya dint 'ear me right, did ya, Shawn?"

There was a new menace in Keith's tone now.

"Erm. I think I did."

"Let me say it again. Kill the cat, ya keep yer job, fine and dandy. But if the cat lives – you don't."

"Erm – right. I don't – keep my job?"

"You don't live."

I thought I was going to shit my pants now. "You mean – you'd – do you mean - *really*?" I squeaked.

"Kill ya? Yep. Without a second thought. Now think on, lad."

Now here was a disciplinary process with teeth.

30. Get Timmy

You can say that what I did that night was unbelievably sick and cruel. You can call me a monster. You can tell me that I'm inhuman for breaking the heart of the girl I love with such a callous act. I know they are all true. I feel as gutted about what happened as anyone else. I'm so, so *sorry*.

Suddenly, I wanted the opposite of what had always been my heart's desire. I so, so wanted to be normal, ordinary, average, even dull. My biggest dream had already come true, I didn't need any of the other stuff. I didn't want to kill a cat, I didn't want to kill people or work for someone who did. I just wanted to be ordinary again. The only thing I wanted more than that was to be with Rosie forever.

What would *you* do? Defy Britain's most notorious professional murderer? Run away from the woman you love? Run away *with* the woman you love – oh yeah, sounds easy. But I knew Rosie was going nowhere – she loved London life too much. I'd be running away on my own, after an explanation that would have killed her blossoming love for me stone dead. Maybe even that would be an option if my heart didn't sink into my guts at the thought of being without Rosie. But Keith would track me down and kill me anyway – that sort of thing would be all in a day's work to him. He had contacts everywhere and a ferocious temper. And he *liked* killing people.

I had no choice. The reckoning hour had come. It was Get Timmy time.

It was surprisingly easy. The first part, I mean. Let's face it, the little fluff monster *trusted* me. He'd sidled up when I was wallowing about outside the flats, gulping in air at the thought of what lay ahead of me. It was too good a chance to miss. Within seconds, I'd scanned the surrounding area, picked him up and bundled him in to the flat. He was quite happy with that. It was a chilly night after all and Rosie was working late at some bash to celebrate Eastbourne – the success of the rescue mission, she assured me, not the scale of the tragedy.

Once in the flat, my task was easy enough. Feed him a bit of tuna to get him totally onside, stroke and fuss him for an hour or so, then take him down to the cellar for more tuna. I'd even got an old heater working and made up a little bed of cushions for him. He was happy as a little sandboy. Shit. Now for the grim bit. *Just grit your teeth and do it, Sean.*

So I did. I really fucking did it. I'm *sorry*.

I stood by the window and waited until she came into view off the bus. She was walking along absently, that half-pissed carelessness about her, and I hated myself. But I had to tell her, I had no choice. One day, maybe, I'd be able to explain. No - I knew that was entirely untrue. Rosie must never, ever find out the truth about this.

I burst out of the flat and ran towards her, legs and arms akimbo. She stopped in her tracks, looking almost afraid.

"Jesus Christ!" I yelled, "Rosie!" And I threw my arms around her.

"Sean! What is it, what's wrong?"

I pulled away from her, shaking my head wildly. "It's horrible. Fucking *horrible*!"

"What? What is?"

We were at her door now. I just stood and gawped at her.

She opened the door silently and I followed her inside. In her living room, she looked at me anxiously and I thought my heart would melt.

"What's happened, Sean? Tell me?"

I sank into an armchair and buried my face in my hands. "I'm really, really, sorry. It's Timmy."

She stared at me. "Timmy?"

I stood up again and put my hands on her shoulders as she looked at me with wide, worried eyes.

"He's been killed, Rosie. I found him … on the doorstep."

Rosie's hand shot to her mouth and her eyes filled with tears. "Oh, no…"

I gulped. "He was . .. in a box. A cardboard box. And his – oh you don't want to know…"

"I do! Tell me what happened to him?"

I was pretty much crying now, too. "They cut his throat. The *bastards*!"

Rosie burst into floods of tears and I felt like the most evil man in the world. No, I *was* the most evil man in the world. I truly was.

And to make matters worse, I agreed to spend the night, comforting her, cuddling her, even making love to her through her tears. Yes, I *know* I shouldn't have gained anything from my monstrous act, but what else could I do? She wanted sex to make her feel better. I wanted sex to make *me* feel better. The inevitable happened, as it were. But it didn't make either of us feel better.

And all the while, the much-mourned Timmy was curled up snugly in my cellar, slurping milk and scoffing tuna to his heart's content.

31. The toast

Politics is such a fickle business, Betsy thought, as Lucy Hammersmith carried over her gin and tonic. They were all there – Ben Hill, Jock Henderson and the oil man himself – all the people who'd wanted to kick her out of the party a matter of days ago. There too were a couple more Shadow Cabinet members, a journalist from the only People's Party supporting newspaper, Guardian Online, and some of Ryan's amateur spin doctor toadies.

Betsy Saunders was the toast of the evening. She'd effectively ended the career of that smug little git Splash and caused the first crisis in confidence in the Government for nearly a decade. Opinion polls had the People's Party trailing by as little as five points, a couple of rogue ones even had them one or two points behind the Coalitionists. This was unchartered territory. Suddenly, papers like Guardian Online were daring to talk of the merits of the plain speaking Betsy Saunders, some even tipping the 'maverick' for promotion to the Shadow Cabinet.

"Here you go, Betsy," beamed Lucy cheerily, though Betsy knew that the upturn in her fortunes was bewildering and infuriating the stupid cow.

Ben Hill raised his glass and puffed on his spliff. "When you said you'd be working against the Coalitionists, we never knew you'd have this effect!"

"Quite," Ryan interjected. "I'm just glad she's on our side!"

The Guardian Online guy was scribbling on his phone. "So Betsy," he murmured, without looking up. "How does it feel to be the toast of the People's Party?"

Betsy took a swig of gin and tonic. "Proves you right, doesn't it?"

He looked up and raised half an eyebrow. "Sorry?"

"Well, a few weeks ago, you said I was toast."

The journo smirked. "A week is a long time in politics."

The last week had indeed been eventful. The furious row in the House, her brief suspension, Richard Splash vehemently denying her allegations, then the TV interview and horrible murder of poor Sadie, then his arrest. He'd clung on desperately to office for several days, denying any impropriety, and then gleefully announcing that Police UK couldn't find any solid evidence against him.

But he was finished politically when another former lover had confirmed he had an unsightly mole on his scrotum. Now no-one believed that he hadn't commissioned Sadie's death, even if it couldn't be proved. Indeed, some of the press were suggesting there wasn't much wrong with that and that the 'antiquated' murder laws were the problem. Others, though, talked of the higher values of politics, the need for MPs to be whiter than white and of the Government's own *Decent Values* campaign. The upshot was a sudden Cabinet reshuffle in which Splash – whose ambition had always been an annoyance to Horace Ronson anyway - was sacked.

Thankfully, the public didn't yet seem ready for politicians being allowed to murder people just like anyone else could. Years ago, they had swallowed the legalisation of murder, the *privatisation* of crime, in return for quite stupendous tax cuts. But nowadays, there were no significant taxes to speak of and people were becoming cynical about the need for politicians at all. They seemed to have a lot of power and influence but to actually contribute very little towards the economy – giving them the right to commission murders would make them dangerously powerful and even less accountable. If they wanted to kill people, then they should give up politics first. Maybe politics had had its time anyway.

While it had been a better week than the previous one, Betsy felt greater despair than ever as she looked around the beaming table. How could these tossers pretend to like her when a week earlier, she'd been public enemy number one? Why did Ryan think that sending her a 'personal note' from the PM would make her wet her knickers – he knew she thought Styles was a complete wanker. And what the fuck would she do if they tried to put her in the Shadow Cabinet? She wouldn't last a week – but happily, she suspected they knew that.

"So, Betsy," said the journo. "Can I quote you on that 'toast' jibe? It's a goodie. And can I get a comment on them not charging Splash?"

"I'm sure we can come up with something," interjected Ryan.

"I know we can," said Betsy. "Yes, you can quote me. Quote me as saying that Sadie's death is a fucking scandal and that no-one really believes Splash wasn't responsible."

"Ah now Betsy, that might be libellous," smarmed Ryan. "Why don't you just say that you've every confidence Police UK will do all they can to get to the bottom of it?"

"Because they won't get to the bottom of it. No, he'll get away with it – he'll lose his career, but that's no fucking loss to anyone but him. Oh, and can you add that he's the most insufferable little prick I've ever met – and believe me, that's up against some tough competition. He even makes Styles look like a decent human being!"

There was a brief, stunned silence, then the table collapsed in a guffaw of contrived, hysterical laughter.

Betsy finished her drink and longed for the honeymoon to be over.

"Same again, Betsy?" smiled Ryan, his eyes blazing with oily irritation. At least they agreed on something.

32. The new assignment

It's surprising how quickly guilt and self-loathing can be brushed aside by practicalities. I woke up hating myself to the sound of Rosie's tears, then shagged her again, then said I had an early start, sneaked next door to feed and stroke Timmy, then set off for work with a spring in my step, ready to tell Keith that I'd finally murdered the moggie.

But when I got there, there was another bloke in the office. Grey, bulky, round-shouldered, he looked a bit like Keith, but shorter.

"This is Archie," Keith announced. "My brother."

Archie nodded gruffly, without smiling. "'Ow do."

"Arhcie's goin' to be 'ere a few days. 'Elpin' out, like."

I don't know why I should have been so surprised. I mean, I'm sure murderers do have families. Maybe it was just that Keith had never mentioned his. Maybe it was the thought that someone like Keith wasn't just a one-off. Who knows, maybe there was fifteen of them.

"Don't look so scared, lad. 'E's not after your job. I just need him for a couple of days. Bit of bisniss."

It was clear that was all he thought I needed to know and he was probably right - I didn't really care to know more. Archie was sitting around the shop reading the paper, so whatever business was being taken care of clearly wasn't happening now. He didn't say a word to me all morning, except for the odd monosyllable when I offered coffee. I took it as a yes and made him one, which he drank without looking up from his paper or thanking me.

Archie's unexpected arrival stole my thunder somewhat and it was lunchtime before I got the chance to engage Keith in conversation about Timmy. We'd sat around all morning in silence, me too frequently checking the answerphones and making coffee, Keith scowling over his accounts, Archie reading his paper and occasionally snorting. A couple of times, he'd mutter something to Keith about the paper and Keith would snort back.

As I made about the seventh cuppa, I thought it was time I raised my triumph with Keith. "Oh, I did that job for you last night," I sang, a bit too casually.

Keith took the coffee and looked at it as if it had sworn at him. "You what?"

"I did that job. Last night."

Keith stared at me for a moment, then registered. "The cat? Did ya?"

"Yep. Just as the lady asked for it. Cardboard box on the doorstep."

My feeble attempts at affecting a casual manner seemed to have attracted Archie's attention. He looked up from his paper, snorted, looked at Keith and smirked. Then he went back to his paper.

"Well, 'bout time," said Keith dismissively, gulping his coffee. "You'll need to move more quickly on this next one."

"Next one?"

"Come in today. Senile old git. Wife wants him bumped off for t'inheritance. Fooxin' saucy mare! Archie and I won't be around, so you'll need to take care of 'im."

Oh God. Yesterday a cat, today an old man. My killing career was taking off at speed.

"Erm – where will you and Archie be?"

"Busy."

"Right…"

Keith picked up a file from his desk. "'Ere you go. This is the fella. Lawrence Fry. Nice old fella probably, but lost his marbles. Wife's a good bit younger and wants rid. Should be a piece o' cake."

He handed me the file. There was this picture of a sweet, gentle looking old man standing outside a big house. And another of him walking down the street, smiling to himself.

"I want this one done right, Shawn. No pissin' about. It 'as to be tonight."

"*Tonight?*"

"Yep. I promised. An' I've never broken a promise in my life. I'd do it myself if I could, 'cos it's more complicated than some. All you need to know is that we don't want the fella's body found. Ever. You'll 'ave to burn the old bastard."

"*Burn* him?!" My voice had risen several octaves on the word 'burn' and Archie snorted again.

"Aye," Keith said. "An' think on. Don't cock it up - we're relyin' on you!"

"But surely there's not going to be any insurance payout if there's no body?" I pleaded.

"Just do as yer told, Shawn."

So there was my evening's entertainment sorted, then. Track down a smiling old man, cut his throat and burn his body. That rejected bar job option kept coming back to me.

33. The suspect

"Sean, do you *have* to go out tonight?"
Rosie pleaded.

She hated it now when he went out. Only
days ago, she'd spent their evenings together
trying work out a way to dump him, to get back
to the friendship they'd once known. But she'd
known it was impossible. Something had broken
that first night they'd slept together and now
there was no going back. The road to platonic
friendship was closed forever. If she dumped
Sean, she broke his heart and ended their
relationship. That was just too big a step to take
– the thought of life without him filled her with
dread.

And there was something more to it as well.
It wasn't just the trauma of losing her beloved
Timmy in such a horrific way. There was
something she was feeling about Sean that she'd
never expected to feel. She'd always seen him
as the perfect confidant, the kindest friend
anyone could have. Ok, she'd always known he
fancied her, maybe even loved her, but that had
never got in the way of him being a great friend.
But that air of the desperado, the sadness he
always had about him when they were together,
had disappeared overnight. Suddenly, he
seemed cool, confident, in control – but still as
wonderful and thoughtful a person as ever.
Maybe she'd just been short sighted about him
before, maybe she'd not been ready for
something like this. But suddenly, Sean was a
different proposition, as easy to love as a lover

as he had been a friend. This was unexpected, but tremendous. Maybe she was falling in love with her best friend – again.

"I'm really sorry. I have to do a job for Keith."

Rosie started. "For Keith? You don't mean…?"

He smiled. "No. It's just a bit of admin. He wants me to run his PR campaign."

"Admin? At night?"

"Well, I said I'd make up the time that we – well, you know!" He grinned sheepishly.

"I wish you'd give up that job. I don't know that I want to sleep with a murderer."

"Don't worry – you're not. Keith definitely sees me as running the business side of things. He does the killing, I do the PR."

She smiled. "Very glamorous, I'm sure. You know, I've been thinking. About Timmy."

He walked across the room and put his arm around her shoulders. "Don't. It's best to try and forget it."

"No, I don't mean that. I've been thinking about who might have had him killed."

He pulled his arm away suddenly and took a step back. "Wh-what?"

"Oh come on, Sean. You should know better than anyone that was a professional job. Your average neighbourhood cat killer doesn't slit throats. It was a professional job. Someone paid for it."

Sean looked a bit afraid.

"Nah – there was no calling card, nothing. I don't think it was professional – not licensed, anyway."

"I'm not saying it was legal. I'm saying someone paid a professional to do it – maybe they wouldn't put it through the books or something, because Timmy was a cat." Her eyes filled with tears. "Poor Timmy," she whispered.

Sean put his arm around her again. "I just don't see it, to be honest. There are firms that specialise in that kind of thing. Why would you take the trouble to pay someone to kill him illegally?"

"So there's no audit trail. If I go to Police UK, they can never demand evidence that he was legally killed."

"But why wouldn't you want an audit trail? Police UK couldn't tell you who'd had him killed anyway if they'd paid for a confidentiality clause."

"But if you were someone who just wanted to cause someone else misery, maybe you wouldn't want the hassle of being questioned about it."

"You're not suggesting…?"

She nodded grimly. "Shirley. I fucking *know* it was her. She hated Timmy -and now she hates me!"

Sean looked startled. "Look, don't jump the gun. You've no evidence…"

"And that's just how the bitch wants it. I've a good mind to get your Keith to slit *her* fucking throat!"

"Hang on, do you really, honestly think that Shirley would do a thing like that?"

The silence between them spoke volumes.

He gave her a squeeze and shook his head. "I honestly think it was just some mad neighbour whose garden Timmy crapped in. But if you really think it was Shirley, well – I can't see it."

"I can. And I'm going to get the bitch for it."

"Get her? H-how?"

"I don't know yet. I don't even know where she lives. But Shirley being Shirley, she won't be able to keep her trap shut for long. She'll either want to gloat about it or use it to try to get back in my pants. She'll be back – and when she is, I'll be fucking ready for her!"

34. Fry Lawrence Fry

The gated mansions of Mare Street stared impassively back at me. I'd never felt comfortable in Hackney. While in Islington there were still people I'd cross the street to avoid, here it felt like people were crossing the road to avoid me. You needed money to live in Hackney and if you didn't positively stink of it, people wondered why you were here – maybe with some justification.

My own mission was hardly innocent. Kill a poorly, confused old man, then set fire to him. I was here to fry Lawrence Fry. The only other non-super rich people in Hackney were probably here on similar enterprising missions – to burgle houses, beat people up or kidnap some billionaire's kid. All perfectly legitimate businesses, of course, but frowned on by the super rich of Hackney who tended to be the prime target of such enterprises.

I looked up and down the street for the umpteenth time. One huge gated mansion followed another, lining Mare Street on either side. Fearsome dogs barked and rattled chains behind the gates, the good folk of Hackney had found their own means of insuring against the legality of what had once been crime. There wasn't a soul in sight now. I'd been here two hours, much of it standing shivering outside 13 Mare Street, or The Gables as it was better known. Home of my erstwhile target, Mr Fry.

I'd googled him earlier, partly in the hope of finding something to dislike. There was nothing. Lawrence Fry had inherited his money from his father, who had in turn inherited it from his grandfather, a 20th century IT boffin and renowned philanthropist. Both Lawrence and his parents had been major donors to charities both at home and overseas and Lawrence had set up free soup kitchens for the homeless and those dispossessed by floods. They were very rich indeed but also very good eggs. Not what I wanted to hear.

Lawrence's wife, on the other hand, was clearly a gold-digging bitch. Thirty years his junior and a former administrator for The Con Merchants, a door to door mugging firm who specialised in targeting old people. There'd been considerable press coverage of their marriage five years ago and Lawrence's insistence that his wife had been "forced into a job she hated through grinding poverty". Well, she was certainly not in poverty now and I doubt there was much grinding going on – other than her plan to have me grind her old man into the dirt.

I looked up and down the street again. A couple of young men were hurrying past, carrying company bags marked 'SWAG', which looked full to the brim. One of them nodded at me, the nod of a fellow tradesman out of place on these wealthy streets. This was no good at all. Lawrence's drive seemed to be the only one not populated by rabid dogs or armed guards, but I couldn't bring myself to try and get inside.

I felt the knife in my pocket and a shudder ran through me. I really couldn't do this. Maybe the best thing was to go home, pack my things and do a runner. But then there was Rosie.

I couldn't leave Rosie. I kept toying with the idea of telling her the truth – it's not as if she wanted me to be a murderer. I could break down, tell her everything, even about Timmy – no, that would be the final straw. She would never forgive me for putting her through that pain, anymore than I would ever forgive myself. And then Keith would probably kill both of us.

"Can I help you?"

The voice in she shadows almost made me leap out of my skin. There was someone approaching me from the other side of the street. In the dark, I couldn't make him out.

"Er, no. I'm just…"

"What's your business here? Murder, is it?"

Well, that was me rumbled. I started to head off down the street. Then the man stepped under a streetlight and I recognised him immediately.

He smiled gently. "Young man, I wouldn't be in your shoes for all the world. I truly wouldn't."

I just stood there, dumbstruck and the old man walked right up to me. He pulled out a pipe, which smelled strongly of cannabis, lit it and puffed away contentedly, still regarding me almost curiously.

"Look, I don't know what you think…"

"I think you came here to kill me. Lawrence Fry." He extended his hand and I took it, not knowing what else to do. He shook me warmly by the hand and beamed.

"Er. Well…."

"Oh, don't worry, I know all about it. Saskia thinks I'm confused." He laughed and leaned forward conspiratorially. "I *am* confused, actually. I don't always remember things from one day to the next. But today is a good day."

"Look," I babbled, "I don't know how you know about this, but you're right. I wish it wasn't true, but it really is. I'm a professional murderer, sent here to kill you. Then I have to burn your body. I'm really sorry!" I gulped in air frantically. I could feel my face reddening and my eyes filling with tears.

"Ah well. Trust me to get the work experience boy, eh?" he chuckled. "I was expecting Keith Hartley to come looming out of the night at me. Never mind!"

And with that, he turned on his heel and headed for The Gables. I ran to catch up with him.

"Hey, hold on!" I felt for the knife in my pocket and my finger found the sharp end. I snatched my hand from my jacket. Spots of blood dripped on to the floor.

Lawrence put his hand on my arm.

"Young man, you're not going to kill me. I know that. I can see it in your eyes. So why not run along home now and get some sleep? Let's not waste each other's time, eh?"

He opened the gate to the Gables and began to walk down the front path.

"W-wait! Please!" I begged. "If I don't kill you, he'll kill me!"

He stopped then walked back down the path, putting his hand on the gate. "Who? Hartley?"

"Y-yes. I'm on – well, a final verbal warning. I didn't kill Timmy, you see. The cat. He's living with me and..."

The old man put a hand on my arm again and looked at me gently. And that was when I started crying. Told him the whole sorry tale, from top to bottom. And all the while he looked at me with kindness and sympathy – the man who'd come here to murder him. He had these piercing blue eyes that seemed to go right through you and just make you tell the truth. He just wasn't what I expected at all.

"Well," he said, when I'd finished my wailing. "I have to admit you're in a bit of a pickle!"

We were standing outside his front gate now and he began to walk back down the street, away from The Gables.

"The sad thing is, I wouldn't mind you killing me. I've lived too long. I don't even mind Saskia getting her hands on the estate. I've no-one else to leave it to and she's had a hard life, you know. The thing is, you're not going to be able to do it – which is fair enough. I couldn't either."

He contemplated me sadly for a while as I hurried alongside him in abject misery. Then his blue eyes lit up.

"The solution's simple! It's the same as it was for the cat. I'll come and live with you!"

I stopped and stared at him. "What? Are you crazy?"

He smiled. "Yes, somewhat. Well, confused anyway. But if you think about it, it's a neat solution. I hole up at your place and talk to the cat, disappear quietly until Saskia declares me dead. You claim you've done your duty to Mr Hartley, then start looking for another job. Saskia gets her money, Hartley gets his, and we all live happily ever after. Sorted!"

And he beamed at me.

"Look, just hold on a minute! That will never work. I have a one bed flat and my girlfriend lives next door. The cat's already sleeping in the cellar. Hiding him is a big problem as it is, the chances of me also hiding you are…"

"Slim," he nodded. "I know that. But I don't mind sharing the cellar. I like cats. And if the worst comes to the worst, you can always just say I'm your grandfather, can't you? And I'll be out of Saskia's hair and she'll be out of mine – frankly, all the amateur scheming to bump me off is a bit embarrassing! No, it's a good solution all round, I think."

"It's not. It's absolute madness!"

He stared at me for a few moments then, that air of playful curiosity still twinkling around him.

"Alright," he said eventually. "Would you care to suggest an alternative plan?"

35. Dead man talking

"Another cup of tea would be marvellous."

Lawrence held out his cup, his eyes still shining. He was clearly enjoying himself. Numerous cups of tea had already been drained and my internal Chancellor of the Exchequer was beginning to get nervous about a teabag-driven economic crisis.

I'd be lying if I said that when Lawrence suggested coming to live with me, the ghost of a thought didn't enter the back of my mind that any money worries I had might be over. After all, the man was stinkingly rich enough for his wife to want to bump him off for the inheritance. But therein, apparently, lay the problem.

"If there's one thing we musn't forget in all of this, it's that I am dead. You killed me, earlier this evening. My body is now burnt to a crisp as per Mr Hartley's orders and everything that I once owned now belongs to Saskia. So I am not here. And I have no money."

My heart sank a bit when he said that. I was already spending a fortune on cat food to look after my previous victim and Keith didn't pay me that well. To now have to support an old man with an apparent tea addiction was going to stretch my finances to the limit.

He seemed to read the thought.

"The alternative, I'm afraid is to go back to plan A and murder me. We can always do that if you prefer?"

"Nah," I gulped. "We don't need to do that."

Lawrence smiled. "I'm most grateful for the stay of execution. I think."

"Tell me," I called from the kitchen, as I refilled the kettle yet again. "There's something in all of this that I don't quite get. Your wife – how will she claim the insurance if there's no body?"

"Oh, I don't about that. Small print was never my strong point. But Saskia – well, you can bet your bottom dollar – or *mine*, actually -," he chuckled. "She'll have it all worked out."

I didn't honestly see how she could, but I let it go – Lawrence clearly didn't know either.

"Now, me being dead – how are we going to manage it? In public relations terms, I mean."

"Public relations? You mean your obituary and all that?"

"No, no, no! I'm not talking about all that nonsense. Though I can't deny it'll be interesting – few of us get the chance to read what people say about us after we die! No, I'm talking about how we keep me – or rather, my continued existence – a secret."

I stared at him glumly. "Well – I did say this never work. I struggle enough keeping Timmy a secret."

"Yes, well a defeatist approach wont help us, will it? I'm quite happy to live in your cellar with a smelly old cat if you're prepared to be a bit discreet! And that means no-one – absolutely no-one – must know that I'm here. The grandfather story is our nuclear option and we should never have to use it. If your friend Mr Hartley finds out, he will almost certainly kill us both."

There was no 'almost' about it, I thought. My cellar was starting to resemble Keith's, except the bodies I was hiding there were alive. And if he ever got even an inkling of that, I most certainly wouldn't be.

36. The corpse

It was four in the morning when I crept out of the house. If it hadn't been for Rosie, I'd have run for the hills and never came back. But love has a many-splintered sting. I was stuck in this increasingly bizarre life because to run away from it would make any life no longer worthwhile. And anyway, I wanted to get to the bottom of the murder I'd just pretended to commit.

All that bloody tea didn't help, but sleep was always going to be a struggle that night. Rosie had been half asleep when I'd called her at midnight, hoping to pop next door and take my mind off the madness around me. So I'd lain awake in bed, wondering how on earth I was going to keep secret a man whose snores could be heard from my cellar. And why on earth I'd been expected to burn and hide his body, which would surely rule out the chances of an insurance claim.

It didn't add up. The more I thought about it, the less sense it made. Having your spouse bumped off for the inheritance was actually against the law, but it was the sort of thing that was difficult to prove – the burden of proof was always on the estate of the bumpee. But I'd seen the contract lying around the office and it was definitely signed by Saskia Fry – surely any lawyer worth their salt could make the case against her stick? And why would you go to Britain's most notorious murderer if it was all

an insurance job, as we in the murder trade call
it?

As sleep steadfastly refused to approach,
this tiny detail of Lawrence's murder began to
obsess me in that strange way things do in the
dead of night. It obsessed me to such a degree
that I got up and smoked a couple of joints. And
then I got paranoid that Keith was involved,
with both the Frys, in stitching me up. Maybe he
knew about Timmy and this was an elaborate
plot to smoke me out. Maybe the monosyllabic
Archie was in on it too. Increasingly unlikely
thoughts tormented me, but it had been an
increasingly unlikely few days.

Eventually, realising that the combination of
crazy thoughts, tea, snoring and cannabis were
not going to add up to sleep any time soon, I
crept out of the flat and headed for the shop. If
Keith and Lawrence were working together, I
was a dead man. I may as well see if the
sentence had been written down anywhere. Or at
least look at the details of the contract Saskia
had agreed and find out what the fuck was going
on.

Aside from a few friendly burglars and the
odd Police UK car, there was no-one about. It
was a twenty-minute walk to the shop, but I was
there in ten. That fear thing can make you run
and I had that fear thing big time. The place was
in complete darkness when I got there – by then
I was in such a state that I'd almost expected to
find Keith and Archie waiting with machetes.

I unlocked the door and stumbled inside. Now, where the fuck was that contract? I 'd seen it out on the table earlier, but now it seemed to have disappeared. In fact, the shop was tidier than it had been for weeks. Tidy, but not clean. There was a fucking awful smell coming from somewhere and it wasn't just my fear. It wasn't stale kebabs either. Where the *fuck* was the contract?

I rooted around a bit, went through the files – there was poor Timmy, seemed the bitch had paid up earlier today. But I couldn't find the Fry file anywhere. Fucking hell, maybe all my paranoia wasn't so wide of the mark? I suddenly felt I needed a drink.

I wandered over to the fridge, still puzzling over that increasingly overpowering smell. Had Keith started burying bodies under the shop?

No, he'd started leaving them in the fridge!!

When I opened that door, I don't know how I didn't keel over and die. The first thing I saw was two dead eyes, staring straight at me.

Crammed into the fridge was the dead body of an old man. He had been placed in a sitting position as that seemed to be the only was to fit him in. I screamed at the top of my voice and I think my arse actually fell out.

And then I heard the door open behind me.

There was a long, stunned silence. Keith and Archie stood in the doorway, staring at me. Archie was carrying a large trunk and Keith seemed to have a spade in his hand. Both looked dirty and dishevelled. And I must have looked petrified. I could feel myself backing away, but there was nowhere to back away to – save for the fridge, which was clearly occupied.

"What the fook are you doin' 'ere at this hour?" barked Keith.

I didn't know what to say. "Just – making up some time?"

Archie chuckled malevolently. They both stared at me.

Then Keith's face tried to broaden into a grin. He walked across the shop, extending his hand.

"Fookin' did it, din't ya? Fookin' *did it*!"

And he shook me warmly by the hand, though my hand was shaking to a different tune. Archie stood in the doorway, still looking at me oddly.

"Thing is, Shawn, yer first one's always the hardest. Even mine was. I know why you've come in 'ere. Admit it! You were gonna look up the contract, try an' find some *meanin'* to it all. Ya were, weren't ya?"

And he hit me playfully around the head and it bloody *hurt*.

"Er – yeah."

I mean, I've heard of the elephant in the room and all that. But for someone to walk in on a man squealing as he discovers a dead body in a fridge and then not mention said dead body is taking the missing of the issue at hand to a whole new stratosphere.

"So you killed our Mr Fry, burned him, then couldn't sleep? Am I right?"

"Er – yeah."

"Fookin' *knew* it! Ya fookin' softie arse!"

And Keith did that mirthless, shaking thing he would probably describe as laughter. Archie smirked along and said something unintelligible to Keith. Cue more mirthless giggles.

"Nah, fair play to ya. I knew you 'ad it in yer! I just knew! You got the madness, Shawn!" And now he put a muddy arm around my shoulder and gave me a huge squeeze. He seemed genuinely excited.

Archie looked past me to the open fridge. "I'll pass on t'coffee," he said, deadpan. "Milk's off!" And off they both went again in fits of silent, wobbly-stomached laughter.

"Well," said Keith. "Now you've blundered in 'ere with yer feelings or whatever, I may as well tell you what's goin' on. Eh?"

"Er – yeah."

And then kill me, perhaps? I really didn't know what the fuck was going on here, but it didn't look good and Keith's new-found bonhomie was positively scary.

"Reight. This old fella in the fridge is one Joe Wallace. I know nothing of him, 'cept he died a couple of weeks ago of natural causes. He left no money and no relatives. Which makes 'im very valuable to us. That's why Archie here took a long time trawling through t'newspapers to find 'im."

"I don't understand."

"I know you don't. But try to work it out, 'cos it involves you."

And he stood there with that strange grimace of his, while Archie raised his eyes to the ceiling and muttered something about them not having all night.

"No, you've lost me," I stammered. "There's a dead man in the fridge, but you didn't kill him and no-one else did. I don't get it."

Keith was clearly enjoying this. "Well think about it. Come on, Lad, you're the one wi' the university education!"

Archie chuckled again, looking at me with even greater contempt than before.

"I don't get...how does it involve me?" It was hard to stop myself from just bursting into tears and running for the door, begging for mercy.

Keith shook his huge head as if in despair and Archie slammed the trunk down in apparent irritation. Keith persisted, though.

"Well – you killed Mr Fry, reight?"

I looked at the floor. "Yeah..."

"Well, Mrs Fry don't want any big delay in her payout, does she?"

He raised an eyebrow. I'd never seen him do that before. A penny was starting to drop with an enormous clang and a giant shudder. The spade. The mud. The trunk. The body. The instruction that Lawrence must never be found.

"You – you dug up ...?"

"By jove, I think 'e's gorrit!" beamed Keith.

"Thank fook," muttered Archie.

"Aye. That were the deal, Shawn. Officially, Lawrence Fry dies of natural causes. His missus finds 'im dead next to her. That's why we're 'ere now. We're takin' this old codger round to Mare Street and she's goin' to cuddle up with him till mornin'. Then she gets some cowboy doctor in to pronounce 'im dead."

"But – this man's been dead two weeks! It'll never…"

"You just 'ave to know the reight doctors. Missus identifies the body, doctor gives death certicate. No-one else needs to get involved - 'E has no other family to speak of. If they call for an investigation later, they'll be excavating Mr Wallace 'ere not Mr Fry – assumin' you've done the old ashes to ashes bit properly? Please tell me you've not fooked it up?" And there was a bit of menace about him again now.

"No" I said airily. "Burnt to a cinder!"

Archie continued to look at me with what I feared was suspicion, but it seemed that was good enough for Keith. He grabbed my shoulder again and shook me hard. "Fookin' *knew* you 'ad it in yer!" And now he really was grinning in jubilation.

"Keith, can I just check? This can't be strictly legal?"

More grunts from Archie and a shrug from Keith. "Course not. Fookin' red tape tyin' bisniss in knots these days! Well, these are 'ard times and 'ard times call for 'ard decisions in bisniss. That's why the contract's been burnt to a cinder too. Can't put these jobs through the books."

I shrugged as well. Having just found a dead body in a fridge, it seemed churlish to get into an argument about the niceties of Keith's financial reporting or the details of what kind of murders were actually permissible.

"Now you get 'ome and get some sleep, fella. You've done well tonight. So me and Archie'll just finish up 'ere and I'll see you tomorrow. Bright an' early, mind!"

I don't think I'd ever seen Keith quite so ebullient. And the fact he had taken my word at face value – that he actually thought I shared his beloved 'madness' - scared me almost as much as poor Joe Wallace had when I'd opened the fridge.

37. The negotiation

Niall Burke was an ugly little bastard. It wasn't just the unwashed hair, scruffy beard, pock-marked skin, black teeth and dirty, bitten fingernails. They didn't help and nor did his tendency to dress like a tramp. But even a well-heeled, perfectly groomed Burke would be an ugly little bastard, thought Splash. Some people just shine with ugliness inside and out. He would feel for the unfortunate sod if Burke wasn't once again driving a ludicrously hard bargain.

"Look, Guv, this is big stuff. And big stuff means big consequences. It's not just that it's against the law. It's that the law are already on to me for the prossie. Another one could see me go down, innit?"

Splash winced at the loudness of the man's grating voice. They were sitting in a drudgy Islington café which wasn't exactly bursting at the seams, but walls had ears when you started to talk about the law and going down.

"That's why I'm suggesting I give you the cash to move abroad once the job is done," he whispered urgently. "But you can't expect me to support you fowever!"

"Not asking you to," Burke replied loudly, refusing to join in the whispering. "My price will prob'ly last me three or four years. Enough to get a new ID and start a new life somewhere else. But it's not easy. I got family here, innit?"

Splash grimaced as the waitress looked over and a man opposite looked up from his paper.

"Please keep your voice down!" he whispered hoarsely.

"Whatever," said Burke and went back to his egg and chips.

Splash sighed. This wasn't turning out to be as easy as the last time. The last time, he'd got in touch with Burke through another MP who'd used him to bump off a couple of aggressive journalists. It had been very straightforward: Burke filled out the forms and dealt with Capital Hitmen for a generous cash payment plus 'expenses' – which Splash suspected were largely narcotic. This time around, the target was one that Capital Hitmen wouldn't touch with a bargepole – officious little oiks that they were. It meant Burke going through the illegal market or carrying out the murder himself – and for that, the scruffy little toe-rag was demanding a cool three million quid. Splash had plenty money, but he didn't want to stump up as much as one million, let alone three.

"Look," he tried again, then lowered his voice. "Look. I am pwpepared to make a final, improved offer. If you awange the killing – or do it yourself – I will pay you seven hundwed and fifty thousand pounds, *plus* expenses. That's up to a maximum of nine hundwed thousand. That's my final offer."

Burke carried on munching his egg and chips. Yoke was dribbling into his beard as he looked up again at Splash, speaking with his mouth still full.

"In that case, there's no deal. I ain't risking prison for a poxy nine hundred grand."

Splash was exasperated. He simply was not paying this little oik so far over the odds, end of story. But how else could justice be done?

"I genuinely can't go any higher than that."

Burke shrugged and carried on scoffing his vile breakfast.

There was a long silence during which Splash considered his options and Burke noisily finished his food. The truth was, the odious little man scared him a little. He knew too much and was just the sort to sell information to a blackmail firm. Even abroad, Splash didn't feel he could entirely trust him. But it was too risky for a man in his position to try to find another Niall Burke. If he kept his nose clean, he still dreamt of returning to the front bench, even to Downing Street. Then he'd get rid of this PC nonsense about MPs not being allowed to have people who annoyed them shot dead.

"Right," said Burke. "I'm off."

"Look, wait a minute!" hissed Splash in his stage whisper.

Burke stood up and pulled on his coat. "Well?"

Splash stared at him with utter loathing. The one weakness of the free market, he thought, was that it was a level enough playing field to allow the likes of Burke to try to hold the likes of him to ransom. It simply couldn't happen. No, let the bastard fuck off.

"I've been thinking. Why don't you get your teeth fixed, you ugly little wunt?"

Burke looked at him with something approaching contempt. "Why don't you learn to speak properly, innit?" And he walked away from the table, pausing at the door to call back. "Bye now, Mr Splash. Hope you get back in the Government soon!"

Cue more wheeling around and scraping of chairs. Splash glowered and went red. That horrid little bastard would pay for this. Christ, now the man who'd been reading the paper was coming across. Please God not one of Rankin's Police UK spooks.

The man walked right up to Splash's table and sat down in Burke's chair. He nodded curtly.

"'Ow do."

"Can I – help you?" Splash said.

"Nah. T'other way round."

The man extended his hand.

"Name's Archie Hartley."

38. Breakfast at Rosie's

Rosie's kiss was long and heartfelt.

"I missed you," she said.

"I missed you too."

Truth was, so much had happened over the last twenty four hours that I hadn't given her much thought – other than knowing she was the one reason I hadn't fled the country screaming.

She looked at me, smiling. "You look tired," she said.

"Yeah. Long night."

I sat down at her table as she prepared us some breakfast.

"What exactly was it that you were doing? Or don't I want to know?"

An image of Joe Wallace's dead, staring eyes burst into my mind and I almost cried out.

She looked up from the breakfast bar.

"Are you ok?"

"Fine. Just tired."

She looked puzzled. "So what was that little noise about?"

Ok, so I did cry out.

"Nothing. Last night was just so boring. I don't want to think about it anymore."

She smiled and carried on beating eggs.

Lawrence had been up bright and early, before me. He was surfing the internet, trying to find out whether he was dead yet.

"I do rather like that cat," he said. "Affectionate little fellow, Jimmy."

"Timmy."

"Yes. Very nice."

He seemed tired today, distracted even. I was slightly worried he'd changed his mind about the whole thing. So before I left for Rosie's, I went out and got him some more teabags.

"You are still ok with our arrangement, aren't you?" I asked.

He looked confused. "What arrangement?"

"Well – you living here."

"Yes," he said vaguely.

"You're sure?"

He looked confused again. "No. I'm not."

"You're not sure?"

He clicked his tongue. "No, I'm not Shaw. I'm Lawrence. Lawrence Fry."

"Er – yes, I know that. But are you still sure you want to live here?"

"You just asked me that."

"I know. Just – making sure."

He smiled then and the twinkle was back. "I'm a little tired today. Lot of excitement for an old man like me. Don't worry about me, Timmy, I'll be fine."

"Timmy? I'm not Timmy. I'm Sean."

Now he looked a bit panicky. "Didn't you just tell me your name was Timmy?"

"No, I'm Sean."

"Don't start all that Shaw stuff again. You're confusing me."

"Not *sure*. Sean."

"You're not sure of your own name?"

"I am sure. I am sure my name is Sean!"

"Oh, don't start with tongue twisters at this time of the day, young man! Why did you say your name was Timmy?"

"No, no. I said the *cat's* name was Timmy!"

He paused, then burst out laughing.

I stood awkwardly on the threshold. I'd promised to have breakfast with Rosie, but was my house guest cracking up after just one evening in my company?

"Yes, that's right. I *like* that cat! Timmy is the cat, you're Sean. It all makes sense now!"

Relief flooded through me and I laughed, too.

"Just wait till I tell Saskia about this!"

My mouth must have dropped open. Then he winked.

"Don't worry. I have good days and bad. But even on the bad ones, I think I will remember my wife has had me murdered!"

"You were miles away," Rosie said, putting down our breakfast.

"Yeah. Just thinking."

"You really do look tired, Sean. Can't you take time off in lieu?"

"Sadly not. Keith wants me in first thing."

She looked concerned. "Just don't overdo it, ok? You've been through a lot recently, with all the shock of what happened to Sara, then finding Timmy. Don't think I don't appreciate what a trauma that was for you as well."

Her eyes were shining with love and concern. I could feel tears of shame prickling at mine.

She put her hand on my face. "You look sad," she said.

A tear was threatening to trickle down my face. The urge to break down and confess everything was overwhelming. Then Rosie's phone rang. She jumped up and fished it out of her jeans. Then she turned it to face me. Staring back from the screen, her eyes filled with leering venom, was Shirley.

39. The stolen strapline

Lee Macken glided out of the car showroom.
The Rolls was a beauty. Not for him any of
those new fangled Microsoft motors. You
couldn't get the parts for them without buying a
whole load of other shit as well. No, Lee was a
classics man and the Rolls was a classic car. To
be able to buy a brand new one had been a
dream of his since childhood.

Business was booming. The NHS deal had
made him a millionaire. He'd been able to
recruit new, state of the art thugs and dispense
with idiots like Malone. Murder businesses were
going into a mini-recession and he'd even had
the legendary Keith Hartley making personal
telephone threats. He didn't know whether to be
thrilled or terrified. He was in awe of Keith
Hartley, saw him as a hero and had almost
wanted to ask for his autograph. But at the same
time, he suspected Hartley was a man who
didn't make idle threats.

Phoning Police UK to report it had made
him sad on one level. He didn't want to put
icons like Keith Hartley out of business. But the
world moved on. And anyway, there'd always
be work for a good murderer. Hartley would just
have to accept a smaller slice of the pie.

One pain in the arse MP. Betsy Saunders,
had questioned his ad campaign and called for
an investigation into how it was funded. But no-
one really cared whether the NHS was getting
into bed with GBH Unlimited. In fact, the

interfering cow had scored a bit of an own goal – already there were plans in place to cut the red tape that held healthcare businesses back. It didn't really matter now whether they did it or not. Lee Macken had made a fortune in a matter of weeks and established a reputation as the leading punishment provider in the UK. There would always be business for him now and he'd made enough money in a matter of weeks to be comfortable for life. Bless Sammy Wonder's strange little arse!

As he stopped at the lights, he gasped aloud. Ahead of him was a huge billboard and on it was his own face, next to that of Keith Hartley.

It read:

WHO WOULD YOU TRUST?

THE ONE WHO LETS THEM OFF WITH A CLIP ROUND THE EAR OR THE ONE WHO KILLS THEM DEAD?

KEITH HARTLEY, MASS MURDERER. *PERMANENTLY* PROTECTING THE COMMUNITY

Lee's good mood disintegrated and he swore as motorists behind him beeped impatiently, then put his foot to the floor. He'd paid a fortune for that fucking *Protecting the Community* strapline when he'd been starting out with very little money. It was his pride and joy. If Hartley thought he could bastardise it, he had another think coming – didn't he know who

Lee *was* now? Sod Hartley being an icon, this was fucking war!

40. So what does he do?

Sean was probably right. She'd been shocked when he leapt up from the table, snatched away her phone and cancelled Shirley's call. She'd then been taken further aback when he'd called the company immediately and had Shirley's number permanently barred from calling her. At the time, she'd thought it was a jealousy thing, but as he explained later, he knew Rosie and Shirley was ancient history.

"It's just that I think she's bad news. She plays games with you. She'll either do all she can to hurt you or she'll guilt trip you. You don't need it."

"I think I'm capable of making that decision for myself!" she'd snapped.

"I don't. She's a dangerous, manipulative cow and you've had a tough time recently. Don't let her back in, even in a small corner of your life. Because it won't stay like that. Before long, she'll be centre stage again – not in the way she wants to be, maybe, but she'll be centre stage."

"What do you mean?"

"She's bad news. If she can't fuck you, she'll fuck you over. Big time."

She'd left it at that. Truth was, she didn't really want to speak to Shirley. She truly suspected her of involvement in killing Timmy. But having her suspicions confirmed – to know for certain that her former girlfriend, who Timmy trusted, had played a part in ending his life – would be too much to bear. Sean had tried hard to dissuade her of the idea – but from his reaction this morning, she felt sure he shared her fears.

"So who's the new bloke, then?" Judy's voice burst into her thoughts.

Rosie was sitting outside the office on one of the corporate benches, eating her sandwiches. She's stopped doing coke at work as part of an attempt to cut down, so she hadn't seen Judy for a few weeks.

Rosie smiled. "How did you find out?"

"Adrienne in your office. Says you keep coming in late and mooning around and that she thinks you have a new fella."

"She's right. Though he's more of an old fella, really. It's my best mate, Sean."

"Awww, how sweet! I knew you'd get over that Ben – he was a right drip! So what's this Sean like, then? It's so sweet that you were best friends before!"

"Well, he's – I don't know. Normal. Ordinary."

Judy's features contorted a little. "Ordinary?"

"Yeah. In a good way."

"Right...and what does he do?"

"Do? Oh, I see. He's an apprentice. An apprentice murderer."

Judy laughed aloud. "You're such a scream, Rosie! I do miss our coke breaks! Why don't you start just doing the odd line again? I won't tell!"

"No. Trying to be good."

"Fair enough. New relationship and all that! So come on, what does Sean *really* do?"

"Erm – well, he – actually, Judy, I wasn't joking. He's a murderer's apprentice. I don't think he does any actual killing, but he does work for a murderer."

Judy gasped and her eyes widened. "Which one?"

"Keith Hartley."

"Oh - my - God!!!" Judy's mouth gaped so widely that Rosie was afraid her brain might fall through it.

"It's no big deal. We don't talk about his work."

"No – no, I bet you don't! It's just – God, what an awful job! You remember that bloke that used to work here – Jake?"

"Jake Johnson?"

"Yeah. Well – Keith Hartley killed him. He was a lovely bloke, Jake. We used to have a right laugh together."

"I thought you hated him?"

"Jake! No, we were really close. I was so sad when he died! I just think that – oh well, each to their own I suppose…"

Rosie said nothing. Not seeing Judy every day had been a major incentive in helping her reduce her cocaine intake. Seeing her again made her realise just how little she had missed her.

"So, this Sean, then. What's he like in bed?"

41. Ongoing investigations

Keith nodded as I walked into the shop. That nod spoke a million decibels. We were colleagues now, worthy of mutual respect. As far as he was concerned, I was a man he could rely on. I was finally a murderer's apprentice. I nodded back, trying to keep it surly.

"How did it go with Saskia?"

He looked at me curiously. "Who?"

"Sask – er, Mrs Fry?"

"Saskia, eh? You two mates, are ya?"

"Er – I just – read her name in the paper. Thought it was unusual."

"What paper?"

Shit, he was interrogating me!

"The contract. You know."

He looked at me again with that slightly puzzled air. "It went fine. No worries."

"Ah. Good."

He shook his head. "Saskia, eh? Fookin' 'ell!"

He was ribbing me. Why the fuck didn't I relax? Why did one strange look make me think he knew that Lawrence Fry and Timmy were living in my cellar?

"Where's Archie today?"

"Fook knows."

"Ah. I thought he was sort of - helping out?"

"'E's my brother. Course 'E was 'elpin'. 'E's a gravedigger by trade."

A gravedigger, eh? The thought occurred that the two could have worked together more often – perhaps they had. One business naturally fed the other, if you see what I mean. But the Hartley brothers were kind of doing it the wrong way round on this occasion.

"So, ow worrit?"

"How was what?"

Keith shook his big head again.

"Yer first murder…?"

"Oh, that. Easier than I'd expected."

He looked surprised. "Fair play to ya, Shawn. You're takin' it all in yer stride. I could never 'ave seen this a couple of weeks ago. You – a mur-derer!" And his giant frame shook again.

"Well, the guy was a bit confused to tell the truth. He walked right up to me in Mare Street and asked me what my business was. I just said 'murder' and I did it there on the spot. Took him down to the old canal and set fire to him. Poor old sod."

He narrowed his eyes. "Old canal, eh?"

"Y- yes…."

He sniffed. "Good spot. No-one asks any questions round there."

He was still eyeing me with a certain curiously. I liked to think it was new-found respect, but there was a part of me that was terrified he could see right through my lies. The only thing that convinced me otherwise was that I was standing there having the thought without my throat cut.

This positively chatty interlude was broken by the door opening. A man and a woman in Police UK uniforms had entered the room. A bored looking middle-aged bloke and a young redhead about my age.

"Oh Christ," said Keith. "Now what?"

"Hello, Sean." said the redhead.

Christ – it was *Miranda*!

Keith wheeled around to look at me.

"Hi," I said. "I didn't know you were – you know…"

She smirked at her colleague, who spoke directly to Keith.

"I've had a further complaint from Mr Macken," he said.

Keith raised his eyebrows. "Oh aye?"

"Yes. He says you, um…" He looked at his notebook. "Oh, yeah. He says you stole his *strapline*."

Keith looked mystified.

"Yes. Protecting the community…he says you've used a version of it and that he's patented the words."

Keith looked briefly perplexed, then pleased. "Ah, well. Advertisin', that. You need to speak to my apprentice 'ere. Shawn deals with all that crap."

And he turned on his heel and walked away, sitting down behind the desk. He picked up a paper and chuckled to himself.

The Police UK guy looked irritated. He looked at me.

"And your name is?"

"Sean Lees," interjected Miranda.

"You two know each other?"

"Intimately, Sir."

He frowned slightly. "Well…what do you have to say about all this?"

"Not much, to be honest. We didn't really steal his strapline. We just sort of – well – took the piss out of it a bit."

Keith snorted loudly. I noticed Miranda suppressing a smile too. Her boss continued to look at his notebook.

"Mr Macken reckons he's patented these words 'protecting the community'. You've used them on a poster. You think that's acceptable?"

"Erm. I hope so. What our poster says is that we protect the community *permanently*. So we're better than him."

"And you protect the community by what? Murdering people?"

Now Keith was back on his feet. "Come on, Lad, you know this is bollocks. I don't know if you're some kinda liberal throwback, but I'm runnin' a legitimate business 'ere. Shawn's telled ya about the ad – we're just tellin' folk if they want a job doin', get it done permanent. Simple as."

The Police UK man tried to look officious, looking again in his notebook. He exchanged glances with Miranda, who seemed to be trying not to laugh.

"Well. That'll be all for now."

"So you aren't going to prosecute us?" I asked. Miranda turned away and walked towards the door. I could see her shoulders heaving. She clearly found all this hilarious.

Her colleague didn't. "We've been paid to investigate whether an illegal theft has been committed. That investigation is ongoing. You'll hear from us in due course."

"Lookin' forward to it, Lad," said Keith.

"And we haven't forgotten Mr Macken's allegation of anti-competitive practices by yourself. That investigation is also ongoing."

"Well, it's good to keep busy," Keith said.

"You'll hear from us in due course." He strode towards the door, catching up with Miranda.

"Bye, Sean," she said. "Nice to see you again." The expression on her face, though, suggested otherwise.

They'd barely left the shop before Keith clapped me round the shoulders. "Great piece o' work, that! Well done, fella. We've riled that fookin' prick Macken good an' proper!"

He rubbed his hands together as he walked across the shop. This new, cheerful Keith was impossible to fathom.

"An' tell me," he added, turning to look at me. "'Ave you knobbed that copper?"

I hardly had time to answer before the door opened and Archie walked in, accompanied by a toady looking little man in a suit. He looked vaguely familiar.

Archie nodded at Keith. "Bisniss," he said and looked at me meaningfully.

"Reighto," said Keith. "Shawn's part of the empire now. You can speak in front of 'im."

The toady man looked at me and then back to Keith. Archie said nothing.

"Well?" asked Keith.

The man extended his hand. "I'm Wichard Splash. Can we talk in confidence?"

Keith frowned. "Shawn does work 'ere."

"Yes, but…do you know who I am?"

"Dick Splash, worrit?"

Splash coloured a little. "Wichard. I deal with MDs only, I'm afwaid. I have a weputation to pwotect. If you want my business – and I will weward you handsomely – I deal diwect with you."

"Ok. Archie – why don't you and Shawn take a walk?"

Archie headed out of the shop and I struggled to catch up with him. It was only about thirty metres down the road that I realised he was actually hurrying away from me. He turned around, looked directly at me, then walked into a pub. I stood awkwardly by the door as if to follow, until he looked at me again from the bar. I didn't know you could tell someone to fuck off without moving your lips, but Archie could.

42. The empty room

The minute I entered the flat, I knew something was wrong. Apart from the excessive tea consumption, you wouldn't always know Lawrence was there. But there was a feeling about the place, a feeling of – well, emptiness. Half a cup of tea lay unfinished on the coffee table. I ran down to the cellar.

There before me was the scene of my worst nightmares – maybe even worse than the nightmares I'd had since meeting Keith. The cellar was empty. The cat's saucer and the bowl I'd bought him as a moving-in-cum-apology present sat neatly in the corner, Lawrence's bed was perfectly made in the centre of the room. But there was no sign of life.

"Timmy?" I called. "Timmy! Ch-ch-ch-ch… Timmy!"

There seemed little point in cooing for Lawrence as well. I looked under the bed and paced around the room. It was indeed empty. *Fuck!* I stood for several minutes gazing around the cellar, willing this to be a bad dream. I wasn't even thinking of what my next move might be. I just stood there. Then my phone rang. It was Rosie and she looked tearful.

"Hi," I said, distractedly.

"Hi. Where are you?"

"In the cellar."

"The cellar? Why?"

"Oh, just – looking."

"Listen, I've just had a really weird experience. I got off the bus and there was a cat that looked exactly like Timmy. He even miaowed at me like Timmy used to do! It's really freaked me out!"

"Er – oh."

SHIT!!!

"Sean, are you *sure* that was him on the doorstep that night?"

"Positive. Don't you remember I brought you his collar?"

She burst into tears, then. Floods of them.

"I'll come round," I said.

Two minutes later, she was in my arms, sobbing. The cat had been so like Timmy and had seemed to recognise her. He'd been sitting on the wall, where he used to sit when she came home from work. It had just seemed too good to be true. And some old man had insisted it was his cat and had picked him up and hurried away. And she'd been convinced the guy was one of those old giffers who groom cats by feeding them and then steal them from you. And...*hang on.*

"This old man. Where is he now?"

"Oh, I don't know. Taken Timmy's twin home, I suppose. I don't care. I just want Timmy back!"

"I know. I'm sorry."

I wanted him back, too. Desperately. What the fuck was that senile old git playing at?

Rosie broke away from my grasp. "Can we eat out tonight?"

"Oh, I don't think..."

"Please? I just want to get out of here for a while."

It seemed I had little choice. "Ok. Let me just nip home and get changed."

"No, Sean. You look fine as you are. Let's just go."

I could seriously have strangled Lawrence Fry. There's an irony in that, I know. I simply couldn't believe that not only had he apparently taken the cat for a walk, he'd also introduced himself to Rosie. How the fuck would I be able to pass him off as my grandad now, when their paths inevitably crossed in future? Rosie had a good head for faces. My mind was racing as we walked down to The Enterprise, the gastro bar on the end of our street. Should I start to introduce him gradually? I decided I would.

"You know, my grandad has a cat that looks very like Timmy."

"Your grandad? I thought he was dead?"

"I mean on my Mum's side. It always struck me how like Timmy he was."

"I didn't know you still had a grandparent alive. Don't you ever see him?"

"No. I lost touch with him years ago. He lives in north London too – somewhere in this area, last I heard."

"God, that's really sad, you losing touch with him. Surely your Mum must have his address?"

"Er, no. They fell out yonks ago."

"That's really sad. That poor old man, living on his own with his cat. He's lost touch with all his family! Sean, I really think you should try to look him up."

"Yeah. I might."

"There's no 'might' about it. And anyway, I want to meet this cat that looks like Timmy…"

Christ, why did one white lie always lead to another. Now we had three Timmys and counting.

43. Cabaret at the Enterprise

The Enterprise is one of those shiny gastro bars full of vacuous people, very 2050. Lovely food, decent service, but certainly none of what my Dad used to call 'character'. I was never quite clear what he meant – he seemed to revel in stories of the old 'pubs' which sounded like wall-to-wall vomiting and fighting fests. He celebrated torn seating, burnt carpets and stained walls, plus rude graffiti in the toilets. He said there was a trend against places that felt 'lived in'. Well, on that, we could agree. The Enterprise is a sterile place, so clean you could almost smell the bleach – the idea of 'lived in' would have appalled 'the Team' there.

That's what they call themselves – the Team. No-one is obviously in charge and they are all relatively interchangeable in how they look, talk and smile. It's a bit like being on board a spaceship from one of those old sci-fi movies my parents used to like. Like everyone has been made into replicas of one another, with the same set of beliefs and mannerisms.

"Good evening," chanted one of the team as we entered. "Table for two?"

He or she ushered us to our seats, pulled out a chair for Rosie and gave us two menus and a company smile.

I delved straight into mine – I was hoping to get through this quickly so that I could make an excuse to go out and hunt down the old man and the cat later. But Rosie sat staring into space.

"Rosie? Are you ok? It's cheaper if we order before seven…"

Rosie nodded meaningfully across the room. I looked round. Glowering at me from a table in the corner was a redhead in a Police UK uniform. Christ, twice in one day – we'd hardly managed that during our honeymoon period! I waved. Miranda nodded, then glared viciously at Rosie. Her date had his back to me, but now looked around. Ah. It was the older copper from this afternoon. Working dinner, then. Poor Miranda. He narrowed his eyes at me, Sherlock Holmes like, and nodded almost imperceptibly.

An uncomfortable hour followed. Miranda's glares were burning into the back of my skull, while Rosie actually began to enjoy herself, smiling across at their table and then laughing conspiratorially in my direction.

"What a sad bitch," she said. "What on earth did you ever see in her?"

Just as we were ordering coffees, the Police UK officers sidled over to our table.

"We meet again," Miranda's boss said, with maximum drollness.

"Hi," I said. "Miranda – you know Rosie. And this is…"

"This is Will," Miranda said. "My boyfriend."

Good God, the bloke must have been twenty years older than her! But still, each to their own.

"Your *boyfriend*?" squealed Rosie.

Miranda looked ready to take her out.

"We've been together a long time," Miranda said. "It was Will who got me my job with Police UK."

"So you work together and play together? How sweet." Rosie liked to push her luck.

"How's the stolen strapline inquiry going?" I asked.

"To schedule," Will replied. Christ, he was an uptight prick.

"As we're now off duty," Miranda said, with a glance at her watch. "Can I just say – I can't *believe* you're a *murderer* these days! I wanted to piss my pants when I saw you in that shop! Have you done any actual killing yet or are you just the one who does the filing?"

"And the ads!" smirked Will.

"I'm only an apprentice," I said. "But my exact role is commercially confidential."

Miranda cracked up at that and the corners of Will's mouth turned upwards too.

"Rosie, can you really imagine Sean killing anyone? He couldn't hurt a fly!" And she laughed again. "I remember one night when…"

"Actually, I've done two so far. If you must know."

That stopped the fat cow in her tracks. It stopped Rosie, too.

"Have you?"

"Yeah."

"I didn't know."

"Well, I don't like to talk about it."

Miranda looked ready to perform a lap of honour. "You didn't tell Rosie? Your best friend? Is that because you're *just good friends*?"

Rosie smiled with mock sweetness. "Actually, we're shagging."

"You don't say. Well, lucky you – just make sure he washes his hands when he comes in from killing people!"

"Thanks for the advice."

"Hadn't we better be going, Miranda?"

"Yeah. Oh, one other thing, Rosie – when he's shagging you and he calls out someone else's name, expect to see them in a bar a few months later. What goes around comes around."

And with that parting shot, they walked away.

Or tried to…but I was just too wound up to let them.

"Don't try and take the moral high ground with me, you tart!" I bellowed after them as Rosie tried frantically to intervene. "I'm not the one who shouts out my brother's name when I'm about to come!"

A stunned silence. And not just from them, standing as though petrified by the door. From the entire Enterprise. Two of the Team were striding towards our table.

"I'm afraid we have to ask you to leave, please," they chorused.

Rosie was already in the process of doing so.

"Here is your bill, Sir."

Miranda and Will were still standing rooted to the spot. Rosie brushed past them on her way out. Conversation was gradually striking up again around the bar. And now Miranda was striding back across the room, followed by Will.

They both had faces like thunder. A member of the Team tried to bar their path, but Will – who suddenly looked two feet taller – cast him aside with a look. Now we were all face to face again.

"What the *fuck* are you talking about, Sean?" demanded Miranda.

"Slander," Will added. "In front of a hundred witnesses."

I wasn't backing down. "You know it's true! You might want to deny it in front of your new man, but I heard what you said that night loud and clear! I wasn't the only one thinking of someone else!"

The Team were now five. "Can we ask you all to leave immediately before we call a police firm?" they sang.

"We *are* a police firm," snapped Greg and pulled out his card.

"Oh," they said in unison and continued to stand there, mouths agape.

"Well come on, then!" yelled Miranda. "What did I say? Do please tell me!"

"Ok!" I shouted back. "You said 'Billy'! You said: *Ooooh, Biiillleeee!*" I was shrieking now and scared I was becoming hysterical.

Silence had descended again. Will and Miranda were laughing. Something had gone wrong here.

"And you thought Billy was my *brother*?"

"Well, he is."

"And you still haven't made any other connection?"

"What?"

The audience was clearly gripped. Not a fork moved. The Team also stood transfixed.

"What is Billy short for?"

"What are you on about?"

"William," one of the Team muttered.

"Thank you," said Miranda. She had gone scarlet, but was now holding court, striding up and down the bar. "Billy is short for William. And can we think of anything else that's short for William?"

"Will!" piped up a voice from the back of the room.

"Thank you. So, Sean. Do you still think I think about my brother during orgasm? Or do you think my *boyfriend* is more likely?"

"Come off it! He wasn't your boyfriend then."

"Just like Rosie wasn't your girlfriend?"

A murmuring in the crowd. They hadn't expected a cabaret, but they were enjoying every moment.

"Yes, but – you didn't even know him then!"

"Oh, Sean. You poor, deluded, fuckwit! I've been sleeping with Will since before I knew you! Before, during and ever since! Did you really think you were the only one whose heart wasn't in it?"

"But…you said 'Billy'…"

"She calls me that," said Will, with strange pride. "When we're … alone…"

Now the crowd was laughing. It was turning into a bad scene from a movie, which would end with a standing ovation. I felt like taking a bow now, saying I'd only been joking all along. How serious was slander? I had no idea.

Miranda was smiling now, somewhat bitterly. "I always liked you, Sean. Even when I saw you today, I remembered the good stuff before the bad. But I didn't know you were such a fucking weirdo that you'd walked away thinking I was shagging my brother! I'm not surprised you've ended up working where you have."

"Where's that?" came an emboldened call from the crowd.

"He's a murderer," Miranda said. "A legit one, but still someone who kills people for a living. And in his spare time, he fantasises about incest!"

"I'm sorry," I mouthed, but Miranda was already heading out of the room, hand in hand with the other Billy she knew. I felt like the bad guy on one of the daytime chat shows on The 24-Hour Chavtastic Channel. I paid my bill in silence and walked out to a chorus of boos. Well, not quite, but it was clear that no-one in there particularly liked me.

44. Walking in circles

The night was still young. I now faced two choices: pursue Rosie and try to make up with her or pursue Lawrence and the cat. It was no choice really. I had to find the old fool before he did any more damage – or caused damage to be done to me.

You would think that looking for a slightly barking old man with a cat – *please God* say he still had the cat – would be a relatively simple task. But wandering around the streets in the dark, I soon began to feel very aimless. Where did I start looking? What if he'd hopped on a bus or tube? Or gone back to Saskia? A shiver ran through me at the thought.

It didn't feel right to ask people. What do you say – 'Have you seen an old man with a cat?' Imagine all the expectant looks, the desire for an explanation of my peculiar quest. No, I just had to wander about in increasing hopelessness, desperately hoping I could see them. I may as well kill two birds with one stone and call Rosie.

"What do *you* want?"

"To say sorry. I shouldn't have lost it like that."

"You made a complete tit of yourself."

"I know. I'm sorry."

"And me."

"I know."

She sighed. "It isn't just that. Do you know what really threw me tonight?"

"No."

"You telling them you'd killed people. I didn't know that. And you told them really boastfully, like it was something to be proud of."

"It wasn't that. I just didn't want them getting one over on me."

"I know. I didn't think you were like that."

"I'm not. Not normally, anyway. It's just that fat ginger …"

"Don't talk about her like that! You were together a long time. I don't want to think that in years to come…"

"I'd never say that about you!"

"You'd never have said it about her once. Aside from the fact that it's blatantly untrue."

She was right. I don't know why I called Miranda fat. She's not even overweight, not significantly anyway. It just seemed to go with ginger. If you're insulting someone – actually, if you're insulting a woman – throwing in the f word always seems to add a bit of venom. So, for the record, Miranda is not fat. She is ginger, though – it was her very striking red hair that first attracted me to her. You know how it is – attributes become negatives, weight is mysteriously piled on – it's a break-up, folks and the bloke is pretending he doesn't care.

"You're right. I shouldn't have said that."

There was a pause. I looked at the phone. Rosie was looking a bit emotional.

"So who did you kill?"

"Erm. Nobody."

"What?"

"I just said that. To win the argument."

"You're joking! What the fuck!"

"It's the God's honest truth. I can honestly say, hand on heart, I haven't killed anyone."

She looked confused. "But you wanted to say you had just to win an argument with an ex?"

"Yeah. I know it's a bit pathetic, but there you go."

"It *is* pathetic," she mused. "But I can't tell you how relieved I am. All evening I've been thinking that I can't go on with this. That I can't go out with someone who kills people for a living."

"Oh. Well, I don't. I'm just the admin guy."

"But you are an apprentice? Presumably, that means that at some point…"

"I think that's what Keith thinks. But it's not for me. I'll have found another job by then."

"I think you should. I didn't realise until tonight how uncomfortable I am with what you do."

"Well, we can't all work for an ethical company like British American Heroin…"

"It's different. The killing is a bit less…direct." She was smiling now, though. "Where are you anyway? You seem to be walking round in circles."

"I am. Just needed some air."

"Well, come home."

She hung up. There wasn't really any point in trawling the streets anymore – I clearly wasn't going to find my two victims. Terror struck me again as a few possible consequences of today's events sailed gaily towards my mind, but I snapped it shut. A night of making up with Rosie would take my mind of my troubles for the time being. Who knows, it might be our last night together before I was executed.

I wandered back to the flats. There was a light on in mine, which was strange – I always turned the lights off when I was out as I knew I could face a hefty fine under the Environmental Crisis Act. *Please say they were home again, safe and sound!*

I turned the key in the lock and opened the door.

Lawrence was standing right behind it.

I nearly kissed him.

"Where the *hell* have you been?!" I asked.

He looked crestfallen.

"I've lost Jimmy," he said.

"What? *How?*"

"Well, I went out to get some teabags and I thought the little fella might like to stretch his legs. He ran about, happy as Larry. Then when I tried to bring him home, he bolted. I'm terribly sorry."

And I'd bought the daft old bastard teabags earlier! I wanted so much to shout at him, but he looked like he might cry.

"Lawrence, I thought we agreed you mustn't go out. And Timmy certainly mustn't. It could put us all in danger."

"I know. I just forgot. It was only when I bought a paper and read that I'd died that I remembered why I was here."

My heart felt like lead in my chest. How on earth were we going to find Timmy now? And what if he went to meet Rosie at the bus stop again? This was all getting out of hand.

My phone rang. It was Rosie, naked. There's some things that can take your mind off almost anything.

45. The late night visitor

It was late at night that Betsy felt most alone. Sitting at home, drinking wine, surfing the net and going through constituents' mail, it was easy to wonder where it had all gone wrong. In many senses, she was a huge success. She'd been elected to Parliament as a People's Party in times that were deeply pro-Coalition Party. She had a national profile, she was fighting for what she believed in, she'd even managed to bring down the most pompous twat in the House.

But something continually nagged at her and told her that now she'd got what she wanted, it wasn't what she'd wanted at all. She was on her own, no siblings, no living parents and very few close friends. Even in the Kellogs House of Commons, her friends were more acquaintances than anything else. What had happened to the fun loving girl she'd once been, with loads of girlfriends and no shortage of boyfriends? When she thought back to her university days, everything had been such a laugh. When did everything become so dreadfully, drearily serious?

Would a change of government make her feel differently? Would she feel then that it had all been worthwhile? It didn't seem as likely as it once had. The People's Party were now supporting so many policies that were anathema to her that it might be even worse, having to defend their record in power. And Styles and co didn't believe in what she did – not remotely. They supported the system as it was, most notably the Enterprise Act, which she saw as the root of so much that was wrong.

Today, she'd received a latter from a woman in her constituency who was being blackmailed over a relationship she'd once had. The blackmail firm were threatening to tell her partner and her teenage children that she'd once had an affair with her partner's brother. The affair was twenty-two years ago, brief and meaningless, but it could destroy this family. The blackmail firm had found out by chance and were making increasingly excessive, unmanageable demands of her. She could no longer afford to pay. She wanted Betsy to investigate whether what they were doing was legal, but Betsy already knew it was. Legal, but not right – in her opinion anyway. But if she raised it with Styles, he'd tell her she was being anti-free market and politically correct. What was the point in being an MP if you couldn't help anyone?

Her inbox was full of the usual mix of heartfelt misery tales like this, junk mail and letters from lobbying groups, most of them barking mad. One came from the Paedophile Society…did she, as the foremost opponent of the Enterprise Act, recognise that the Act was wholly inequitable? Did she support their case for reform of our antiquated laws about having sex with children? The fact that the Act had expressly forbidden an activity which not only had a huge potential market, but also catered for the perfectly natural desires of a persecuted minority, surely showed it had no place in a democratic society? Once upon a time, homosexuality and gender dysphoria had been similarly despised by a bigoted and ignorant majority. Surely now, in the 21st century, it was time to stop the witch hunt against the sexual preferences of a small minority? Betsy sighed deeply and deleted the email. She downed her red wine and got up. There was little point in sitting here getting depressed. She may as well go to bed and go to sleep depressed.

Just as she went to turn the living room light out, there was a tap on the front door. Visitors at this time were unusual, but not unheard of – but rarely good news. As an MP, you had to be careful – occasionally, you'd get people turning up drunk and abusive, or even physically threatening you. She went to the door and looked through the peephole. As she did so, there was a moan and an enormous crash on the other side of the door. She could see nothing, but she could hear someone who sounded like they were in pain. Without hesitation, she opened the front door.

Lying on the garden path in front of her, clutching his shoulder, was a huge, greying man. He was grimacing and struggling for breath. Next to him, she noticed with sudden horror, was a large kitchen knife.

"Are you alright?" she called. "Have you been attacked?"

The man was going purple as she spoke. Heart attack, she suddenly realised, and ran inside for her phone. There was no point in dialling 999 and listening to umpteen recorded adverts from the various competitors – she got straight on to the Whittington Hospital.

"I'm sorry," a snotty woman told her. "We're full up tonight. Do you want to try Homerton?"

There simply wasn't time. Betsy ran outside, kneeled on the floor and performed mouth to mouth on the stranger. It seemed to help, he coughed and spluttered a bit, then passed out. She was at a loss for what to do – was this man going to die on her doorstep?

Then a car pulled up outside and another large-framed man got out. "What's to do?" he asked.

"I think this man's had a heart attack! I'm not sure he's breathing!"

The big man looked very concerned and hurried over. "Keith!" he shouted. "Keith!"

There was no response. Without more ado, and without a word to Betsy, the man bent down and, struggling valiantly, hoisted the other man on to his shoulders. Teeth clenched with the effort, he carried the man down her garden path and bundled him into the car.

"Wait! Wait a minute!" she yelled after him, but the man slammed the car door and took off at speed. The fallen knife remained in her garden. Betsy picked it up, took it inside and closed the door.

46. Whiskey with Rosie

Whiskey. It was sometimes the only way to get to sleep. Rosie sat in her living room and sipped at her third one. Sometimes, it was a good way to stay awake too.

There was no doubt about it. Her and Sean clicked physically. She'd gone into all this via a moment of madness and unsure of her own sexuality, but there was no questioning the fact that when they were in bed together, sparks flew. It was almost the antithesis of what people told you about sleeping with a friend – that it would be awkward, fumbly, inhibited. It wasn't. It was quite Something Else.

Whether her judgement was being clouded by the sheer joy of what had happened an hour or so ago – several times, but it had stopped about an hour ago – it was hard to tell. But Sean had hurt her tonight, first with what now seemed to be a white lie about his killing career, then much more with his very emotional reaction to Miranda's jibes. And that had been the real hurt. Sean had been continually dismissive of Miranda and their relationship, he'd called her fat and ginger when she was actually pretty – but somewhere within him was a seed of anger and pain about her. It made Rosie feel that for all Sean's love for her – and she didn't doubt that had been there for a long time – he had the capacity to rewrite history and change the facts of his feelings at a stroke. Maybe that meant he was more cut out for murder than he thought.

How much did that bother her – what he did for a living? Should it bother her at all? She'd never really given it a second thought in the past, except to be girlishly excited that he was meeting someone as famous as Keith Hartley. Even when they'd started seeing each other, she hadn't given it any more thought. But her conversation with Judy and the one in the Enterprise earlier had convinced her that it was something about Sean that she wanted to change. Some people saw murder as a glamorous profession, a bit like being a fireman (though usually with the opposite consequence.) But to most of the people she knew, it was a dirty, horrible job that required a brutal, uncaring nature. It didn't fit her Sean at all and she didn't want other people to think that it did.

Her Sean. It was still hard to believe she was calling him that. How had she gone from thinking about him as a sweet, dear friend with delusions of sleeping with her to 'her Sean'? Things had happened so fast. Shirley gone – *cat-killing whore!* – Ben gone – and Sean had somehow filled the vacuum. In fact, he'd made her realise that there had *always* been a vacuum and a huge one, even when Shirley and Ben were swirling around inside it.

She poured a fourth one. Why had Sean decided to become an apprentice to a murderer? It was such a very bad fit. When he'd first told her, she'd been surprised and laughed quite a lot. Now, the more she thought about it, everything about his job went against his nature to a quite alarming degree. Sean was warm, caring, funny, something of a clod at times. But Miranda was right – he didn't have a vicious bone in his body. Yet he'd walked up to Britain's most notorious hired killer and asked him for a job – and got one. Why the fuck had he done that?

Maybe it said more about Sean than anything else. Ever since she'd known him – even when he'd followed her lapdog-like around Uni – Sean had been *ordinary*. Not dull or boring – just ordinary, average, normal. It's rare that a trait of ordinariness is something you notice in a person – usually, it's the wacky, out there bits of people that attract you to them. But Sean's normality had a pleasing sense of steadiness about it, a reassuring quality that had helped her through some chaotic and emotional years.

Was he himself aware and unhappy that that was how he came across? Had he become a murderer's apprentice just to make himself a bit more exotic? If so, she wished he hadn't. It didn't work at all – it made him somehow incongruous, less comfortable in his own skin. When he talked about his job – and she realised now that he very rarely did – he seemed outside his comfort zone. Awkward, embarrassed, like he had things to hide. And it wasn't just social embarrassment – no, she decided, a very big part of Sean hated what he did for a job. But another part of him would equally hate giving it up and doing something more average, something that would tick the final box in his 'ordinary' portfolio to the point where someone would shout 'HOUSE!"

Get her and her psycho-analysis. It was easy for her to be critical. She hated her own job with a passion, it was a convenience, something to pay the bills. She knew her employer was unethical and she knew that ought to bother her a bit more than it did. The thing was, everything was unethical these days. Unless you wanted to become a prissy protester against everything like Sara and her mates, you would probably always be doing something your grandparents' generation would be appalled by.

The world is mad, she thought as she poured another drink. Maybe it always had been. Maybe people had always had to spend their lives doing things they didn't want to, simply to make ends meet. Maybe there had always been people like Sean, doing wildly unsuitable things with their lives and hating every minute of it, just to make themselves feel more interesting and glamorous. And then there were people like Keith Hartley and Howard Clarke, who were just born to do what they did and knew it. But who would she rather spend an evening with – Sean or one of those two freaks?

She resolved again to redouble her efforts to get Sean to change jobs. Maybe she would do the same. Already, she was facing the prospect of going in to the office with another hangover and doing next to nothing and at the moment, she didn't care. What was the worst that would happen as a result? Surely there must be jobs out there that people actually enjoyed? Maybe she and Sean could go into business together, doing something nice and fluffy?

She downed the whiskey and smiled. If they were as good in business together as they were in bed, they'd be millionaires. Yes, there was no doubt about it – Rosie and Sean clicked physically. She switched the light off and stumbled towards her bedroom, wondering whether it was worth waking him just to prove that point again.

47. Archie's orders

There was no doubt about it, me and Rosie clicked physically. There was just something awesome about having sex with her. I was mooning around thinking about it on the way to work, trying not to get aroused in the street. It just *worked*, I thought gleefully and I beamed as I walked into the shop. Archie – who was standing alone behind the counter – didn't beam back.

"Morning, Archie. Where's Keith?"

"E's 'ad 'art attack," he responded bluntly.

Well, that stopped me in my tracks. I stopped in the middle of the room and stared at him.

"He's what?"

"You 'eared. 'E's in 't'Homerton."

"Shit. I'm sorry. Is he…is he going to be ok?"

Archie shrugged.

"Can I go and see him?"

"It's a free country."

It was like getting blood out of a miserable bastard. Archie continued to stand there, looking back at me glumly.

"So…do we close the shop, Archie? I don't know."

He sneered at me then. "You don't know? Thought you were our Keith's apprentice?"

"Yes, but…"

"So get to work. There's orders 'ere to be done. And you need to care of another one that's not going through t'books."

"Really? What's that one?"

"MP. Betsy Saunders. Keith keeled over tryin' to do her last night. You need to get it done quick before she squeals."

My heart was pounding as he spoke. What the fuck was this about? The murder of MPs was highly illegal even under the Enterprise Act. In fact, it was one of the key stipulations of the Act that sitting politicians could not be targeted as it may damage the democratic process. Not everyone agreed with it and there was no doubt some people stood for election simply as an insurance policy, but to murder an MP was a serious crime. Was this the confidential business that Splash guy was on about?

"Archie, that's completely illegal!"

He shrugged. "Why'd you think it's not in t'books?!"

"Well, I can't do that! I can't kill her. I could go to jail."

"Look, Arsewipe, yer doin' it. End of story."

He strode out from behind the counter as he spoke, looking threatening.

"But that's not fair…!" I began, until his faced creased with laughter.

"'That's not fair! That's not fair!'" he muttered. "Listen to yerself!"

"Look, Archie, I'm sorry, but this isn't my job. I won't do it."

"Won't ya?" Archie resembled Keith more and more when he got annoyed.

"No. Look, if it's that important, why don't you do it?"

He looked genuinely shocked. "What d' ya think I am, a bloody mur-derer? I just 'elp out. Murder's Keith's job. An' yours."

There was a long silence while I thought about all he'd said and he glowered at me. I knew who Betsy Saunders was and I knew there was every chance that what had happened could put Keith in serious trouble. I didn't want that. But then, maybe I did. Maybe this was the chance I was looking for. If Keith got sent down and the business collapsed, I could be completely off the hook! I took a deep breath.

"I'm not doing it, Archie," I said.

"Right.. In that case, be scared. Scared for that lass yer knobbin', scared for that sister you got!"

"What?! What the hell do you mean by that?"

He smiled coldly, with intent.

"You just said you don't kill people…"

"*I* don't. But I've plenty cash."

This was turning into a really shit day – and how the hell did he know about Rosie, let alone Sara?

"How do you know all this about me?"

He shrugged again. "Like to know who I'm dealin' with. Our Keith's a shite judge."

"So …you've investigated me?"

"Yer whinin' again…"

He plonked a card on the desk in front of me. It read 'Rick Rooney, Private Detective'. The bloke's shop was on the end of this street – he was a strange looking little man with dark glasses and a moustache. He should have been easy enough to spot if he'd followed me home, but then I'd been away with the pixies for weeks.

"But why would you do that?"

"Simple. I don't trust you. Keith's too trustin'. That were the problem when we were lads. That's 'ow 'E ended up like 'E did."

"What happened?"

"Let's just say we didn't all 'ave your cosy upbringin'. Now think on!"

Christ, Archie was a tougher proposition than I'd ever thought. And if he'd investigated me through a detective agency, how much did he actually know? If I'd been followed, he might know the whole truth about Timmy and Lawrence…! Shit a fucking *brick*…!

No, I was panicking. If he'd known that, he'd have come right out and told Keith. And everything Rooney had told him you could find out on Facebook or Google. But it was clear that Archie knew where I lived, as it were.

"I don't seem to have any choice," I said. "But this is never going to work. She'll have increased security, CCTV, Police UK…how I am supposed to kill her?"

The shrugging was getting irritating. "Not my problem."

47. Pouring trouble on oily waters

Betsy was scared.

Not just scared, terrified.

All her life she'd been a woman of principle, someone prepared to stand up and fight for what she believed was right. But the man with the kitchen knife had changed all that. The more she thought about it, the more she knew he'd come to kill her. Whether he was a lone nutter or someone being paid for the job, she didn't know. She knew that she could get Police UK on the case to find out if any laws had been broken, but at the moment all she felt was fear. Somebody wanted her dead and that thought was more frightening than anything she'd ever known before.

She sat in Ryan's office, waiting for him to finish what he obviously wanted to make clear was a much more important call. He'd already been on the phone ten minutes, discussing the spin the opposition could put on some Coalition MP who had called for the age of consent to be reduced from 14 to 11. They didn't want to appear draconian and old-fashioned, but equally they didn't agree. Eventually, finally, he put the phone down.

"Sorry about that," he oiled. "Bloody Coalition backbenchers!"

She nodded.

"So…what can I do for you, Betsy?" He leaned back self-importantly, then seemed to spot something. "Hey…are you ok?"

Betsy wasn't. Hot, fat tears were starting to streak their way down her cheeks. *Shit*! If there was one person she didn't want to lose it in front of, it was Ryan. But she couldn't help it. And as he got up and slid round the desk, the fat tears turned into fat, lunging sobs.

"Betsy, Betsy, Betsy!" he smoothed. "What *ever's* the matter?"

He had the air of one of the old 20th century priests she'd read about. Waiting for a devastating confession, waiting to offer forgiveness in return for penance – or a quick blow job, if she was a young boy. The only thing that broke up her sobbing was the realisation that the oil man thought she'd come here to confess some misdemeanour. And that he was relishing the thought.

She stopped and composed herself. "Last night," she said waveringly. "A man came to my house with a knife."

Ryan looked mildly shocked.

"He knocked on the door, but when I opened it, he had fallen over. I think he had a heart attack."

Now Ryan looked perplexed. It was like he'd worn the wrong frown for the weather of this conversation.

"The more I think about it, the more I know that he came to kill me."

"Right," he said vaguely. "Right. You think he came to kill you and then passed out?"

"I'm sure of it. He had a ruddy great carving knife in his hand."

.   "That's not really a conclusive case, though, is it? I mean, he *may* have come to kill you, but we don't *know* that."

"I do. Another man came to collect him in a car. When he realised what had happened, he just carted him away without a word."

"Right. So you think – well, what do you think? An unlicensed murder? A raving constituent? What are you saying here?"

"I don't know. I just think he came to kill me."

"And – with the greatest sympathy for what you went through last night – what do you want me to do about it?"

"Well – for *fuck's* sake, Ryan – don't you think it needs investigating?! A man in an MP's garden with a knife in his hand? It doesn't worry you?!"

"It does, a little," he said. "But without knowing who he was and why he was really there –

I mean, there could be hundreds of innocent explanations."

Betsy was gobsmacked. "Hundreds? For a man knocking on my door in the dead of the night with a knife in his hand?"

"I think you may be jumping to conclusions. Or you may not be, of course. You could always ask Police UK to investigate?"

"That's what I thought *you* might do!" Betsy spat back. "Unless it was you bastards sent him!"

As soon as she said that, she regretted it. Ryan's face clouded over with annoyance.

"That," he said slowly. "Is the final straw. You come in here asking me to help, then you accuse me of trying to have you killed. I'm sorry, Betsy, but I think you're completely insane. Insane, and unsuitable for office. I'm withdrawing the whip."

"Look, Ryan, something pretty traumatic just happened to me…!"

His eyes were granite in his oily face. "I don't give a shit, Betsy! I am sick to death of being demonised by you. If you seriously think that a Party you joined and continue to represent wants to kill you, then I think you have finally gone completely off your rocker! I don't want you in my party and I don't want you in my office!"

"Hang on," she pleaded. "We've got off on the wrong foot here…"

But Ryan had already picked up the phone. "I'm busy," he said brusquely.

48. Meet Grandad

I was starting to dread coming home. As soon as I put my key in the outside door, something, somewhere, told me something was wrong. It was the sound of voices from my flat that ratcheted things up towards a red alert. And it was the sight of Rosie and Lawrence facing each other in the two chairs in my living room that sent my heart scarpering back to down the road to have a pint with Archie.

Silence fell. It fell like it falls in movies, that horrible, huge, gaping silence that doesn't actually happen in the real world. Except in mine.

I looked from one to the other and they looked at me. Then Rosie spoke.

"Look who's here!"

I looked from one to the other again.

"Cat got your tongue?" beamed Lawrence.

"Cat?" I said dumbly. "Sorry."

Rosie looked at me and – she wasn't angry. No, she was smiling. What the fuck was going on? Why did I feel, increasingly, that I never knew what the fuck was going on?

"Don't you recognise your grandad?"

Lawrence beamed again. "Hello, Sean! I thought I'd look you up!"

Ah. Now I don't know how the old fool had done this, but...it was ok. For now.

"How lovely to see you! It's funny, I was only talking about you the other day!"

"Yes, young Rosie here told me! I was on my way to see you the other night, but made the mistake of bringing Jimmy, because I remembered you liked cats. But he ran off and then Rosie thought he was hers. It was all a bit confused!"

"Wow. What a coincidence."

"Isn't it?" Rosie said and I tried but failed to find a hint of sarcasm. "Your grandad's cat, who looks just like mine, sits exactly where Timmy used to meet me. And he's called Jimmy, which sounds like Timmy. And then I turn out to be your next door neighbour and your girlfriend. Amazing!"

My *girlfriend*...wow!

"Yes, amazing. So how did you get here, Grandad?

Lawrence looked confused and that scared me.

"I saw him outside," said Rosie. "I recognised him from the other night. It turns out he still hasn't found his cat."

"That's right," said Lawrence, rather too quickly. "I got up first thing and I knew you'd be pleased if I could find little Timmy, so I went to look for him. Thought it'd be a nice surprise when you got home."

"You mean Jimmy, not Timmy."

"Do I? Yes, I suppose so. I thought you told me his name was Timmy? Lovely cat, anyway."

Now it was Rosie's turn to look confused. And time for me to interject.

"It's been a long day for you, Grandad, coming all the way over here. Do you want to have a lie down?"

He looked a bit panicky now. "Yes, I can go down to the cellar for a sleep if it would help."

"The cellar!" Rosie laughed. "No, have a lie down in Sean's bed. He won't mind."

"Of course I won't, you don't need to trail down to the cellar!"

"Well, that's very kind. Though there's no need. I rather like the cellar. Quite cosy!"

Rosie was looking from him to me now. Confusion and bewilderment were bouncing round the room, like a ball passed from one of us to the other.

Lawrence stood up. I immediately took his arm and steered him though the living room, through the kitchen and into my bedroom.

"Lawrence!" I hissed. "What on earth are you playing at?"

He looked disappointed. "Oh. Thought I'd done rather well. Especially when she heard me outside calling Timmy. Coming up with that alternative name was a stroke of genius, I thought! And as for that cover story about being your grandfather – always thought people would swallow that one!"

"But…what were you doing outside?"

"I told you. I went to look for Timmy."

"Yes…you told Rosie as well!"

"Did I? I'm sorry about that."

"Look, Lawrence, if this is going to work, you just have to stay indoors! You can't be wandering around the streets of Islington every day. You're meant to be dead!"

"Ah, yes, I keep forgetting that. I'm sorry."

"Well, just stay in here now. I'll try to smooth things over with Rosie."

He looked sad and I felt awful, but what could I do? He was putting both our lives at risk on a daily basis.

282

49. The Hackney Messiah

The bed looked too small for him. Keith lay there, wires going in and out of him and a machine behind him monitoring his heart rate, looking uncomfortably packed in and restrained. He nodded with his eyes as I came in. He was sitting up in bed, looking annoyed. He didn't try the smiling thing.

"Well, how are you?" I asked jovially, as if I'd bumped into an old mate in a bar.

He scowled. "'Ow do you think I am? I'm in t'hospital."

"Yeah. I'm sorry. Brought you some grapes!"

Grapes have since time immemorial been the perfect gift to bring to people in hospital. Fuck knows why. They have an annoying moreishness about them which makes you eat them when you don't want to, then shit them out when you don't want to. Whoever decided they were the ideal thing to bring with you when visiting a hospital patient didn't have to clean the sheets.

Keith clearly shared my view, ignoring the grapes and leaning forward conspiratorially. It took an embarrassing few seconds before I realised that he was expecting me to lean in so he could whisper. He scowled again and I hurried forward.

"'As Archie told ya about that MP?"

"Yes. I'll do it as soon as I can."

"No time like t'present. She's a gobby cow, that one, wi' all sorts of fookin' weird ideas. Get it done now. I'll sleep better when you 'ave."

"Ok," I sat down. "I'm on it."

"Yer on what? Yer fookin' arse, as far as I can see!"

"Ha ha, yeah! No, I'll do it as soon as I leave."

"Reighto. Off you pop, then."

"Well, hang on – I did come to visit you and see you were ok…"

"Aye, well you've seen me now. An' you'll be seein' me in jail if you don't get Blabbermouth sorted!"

I stood up. "Ok. I'll do it."

"Good. An' get my fookin' knife back if ya can. It's a beauty, that one."

Despair gathered around my bones as I shuffled out of the ward. As I did so, I heard a little gasp to my left, where the nurses were seated. A young black man with a mohican haircut, wearing a doctor's coat with silver buttons, had entered the room. NIKE was emblazoned across this chest and he wore a baseball cap saying "Sponsored by Coca Cola."

I suddenly realised who he was, as you tend to do when you spot famous people and vaguely think you know them. This was Dr Ronaldo Barnes, the first doctor to be transferred between hospitals for a fee of a million pounds. Was he actually treating Keith? He brushed past me, followed by two aides, one carrying his bag and the other a set of papers – and headed straight up to Keith's bed. I lingered in the doorway, by the armed guards.

Dr Barnes held up his hand and high-fived Keith, who managed a strange cross between grumpy and slightly star-struck.

"So, how goes it, Mr Hartley?"

"It goes alright. Will go better when I'm outta here."

Dr Barnes smiled and I almost had to take cover from the gleam of his teeth. They must have cost a fortune, but when you're earning two hundred grand a week, that wouldn't matter.

"You've only been here a day yet. We'd like to keep you under observation for a little while longer."

Keith grimaced, then caught my eye. He looked as if he were about to get out of bed and bodily remove me from the ward. Dr Barnes followed his gaze. He smiled.

"Ah, autograph hunter, I think!" He pulled out a solid gold pen, then hesitated. "Oh now, hang on – whose do you want? Mine or Mr Hartley's?"

Keith raised his eyes to the ceiling.

"Er, yours…" I said meekly.

Dr Barnes pulled out an embossed pad from the pocket of his white coat. The paper was glossy and had the Nike and Coca Cola logos on it, together with a small inset picture of himself. He scribbled on it, tore out the page and handed it to me. He had signed his name above a mini-strapline, which read: Dr Ronaldo Barnes. The 'Hackney Messiah'.

"Thanks very much!" I said and backed out of the room, trying to escape Keith's disgusted glare.

50. Betsy's party

Betsy was drunk. Horribly, incoherently, irresponsibly drunk.

She'd sat in the Kellogs House of Commons bar drinking all afternoon after her altercation with Ryan and then she'd rung up Styles' private office and told them they were all wankers. Now she was home and had hit the gin. It wasn't even five o'clock yet and the bottle was empty.

She got up and half-staggered across the room. Shit, she'd drunk a lot. But she needed more. Suddenly, the world looked a dark place and one Betsy didn't fit into anywhere. All her ideals and principles were no good when she was shit scared and no-one agreed with her anyway. And why had she got in a row with that oily twat today? Sometimes even she thought she was a bit of a loose cannon. She pulled on her coat, made a half-arsed attempt to straighten her hair, and headed out for the off-licence.

She'd reached the end of her path, when she nearly walked into a nervous-looking young man who was standing there. She jumped back, frightened, then realised he looked pretty normal. He had an ordinary, harmless look about him. Still, you couldn't be too careful these days.

"Hello," she said. "Can I help you?"

The young man looked vaguely distracted. "Er, no. I'm just...you know. I'm just looking."

"Looking?"

"Yeah. Looking for my cat. Have you seen him?"

"What does he look like?"

"Oh, he's lovely."

Betsy frowned and tried to sober up. "Lovely?"

"Yeah, he is. I hope I find him! Well, nice talking to you!"

And the strange young man hurried away. He may have looked ordinary, but he clearly wasn't.

Betsy pulled up the collar on her coat and hurried to the off-licence on the end of her road.

"Betsy Saunders!" Raj greeted her enthusiastically. "How are you today?"

"Oh, I'm alright, thanks. Can I get a litre of NatWest Gin please, Raj?"

"Sure. I heard about you on the radio today. Did you get fired or something?"

"Not exactly."

"Ah! So you're still my MP!"

"I hope so."

"That's good! Because there's something I want to talk to you about. This new increase in poll tax. I don't agree with it at all!"

Betsy handed over her credit card and took the litre of gin from him. "Me neither. I voted against it."

"Against it? But I thought the People's Party were in favour of it?"

"Not all of us. But there's not a lot I can do on my own."

"But you're on your own now, aren't you? No party?"

A party on her own. It hadn't even occurred to her, though it was sort of what she'd spent the day doing.

And that was when the spirit of the old Betsy started to rise up briefly again. Where would people be if she didn't stand up and fight for what she believed in? If all the People's Party meekly toed the party line and waited for jobs in she Shadow Cabinet? Where would Parliament be if there was no-one to oppose the Enterprise Act, exorbitant poll tax and all of the other things Gregory Styles seemed to agree with? Why was she letting one madman with a knife and one oily rat with a persecution complex derail her?

She beamed at Raj, who took an involuntary step backwards.

"The best parties are often on your own!" she slurred slightly, before turning to leave the off licence. She could sense him staring after her.

51. An assassin waits

Standing outside another big house, shivering. Barnsbury Street was the address I was given and here I was. How the fuck had my life come to this? Why was I standing outside the home of one of Britain's best-known politicians, with a carving knife in my inside pocket and an incessant thumping, jumping movement in my heart? Surely a bar job would've been easier than this?

It was a pretty house, what they call 21st century Victorian, i.e purpose built in a Victorian style, using similar kinds of brick, except the bricks were now made in dedicated factories. The front garden was pretty if a little unkempt, flowers had been planted but not particularly well-tended and it was on the verge of getting out of hand, but the bright colours gave it a vibrant feel.

I'd nearly passed out when she'd come out of the front door. I'd recognised her immediately and I don't know why it was a surprise to me that Betsy Saunders should walk out of her own house. And what was all that bollocks about cats? Did I have some kind of verbal tick that made me mention cats whenever my nerve failed me? I shuddered as I remembered asking Rosie about taking the cat for a walk and Shirley's surly response. Cats don't do walkies indeed – but you can always behead them.

I could see Betsy again now, sauntering up the road. She was carrying something – a bottle? Christ, she was waving it about like a watering can – was she pissed? She'd only been gone a couple of minutes. Maybe she was already pissed when we'd met earlier and I hadn't noticed. Here was a newspaper story waiting to happen, I thought excitedly. Then I realised that her sudden murder would be far bigger news.

But let's face it, that wasn't going to happen. I was standing there with the knife in my coat, but I was never going to use it. I'd told myself I would, convinced myself vociferously that I had to. Archie's threats to my loved ones were the big driving force that would finally turn me into a killer. But as I watched her stagger in my direction – she really *was* pissed – I knew I couldn't do it.

I stood staring at the ground. As I stared, a big spider went scuttling past. Christ, it was that big it nearly had shoulders! What an easy life those little bastards had, I thought. No worries, no demands on you and the worst that could happen was you got flushed down the plughole – whereupon you just climbed up again.

No, sod that, the worst that could happen was being stood on and crushed to death by a drunken Member of Parliament. Yep, Betsy carelessly ended his scuttling, flushing, carefree existence forever without even knowing it. If only I found killing that easy.

She was looking at me now, with hazy suspicion.

"You still here?" she slurred.

"Yes. Still looking for the cat. Ha ha."

She looked at me for a moment, then brushed hurriedly past. Or tried to. The pavement was a bit narrow here because her garden had been extended to take up half of it. I tried to step back to let her past, honest I did, but somehow or other I managed to leave a leg outstretched...

It was sheer luck or the worst luck in the world, depending on how you looked at it. Betsy Saunders MP went sprawling over my leg, arms and legs akimbo. Her bottle of gin flew up in the air and landed on the roadside with a tinkling, splintering CRASH. She went head first into the garden wall and the bang was almost as loud as the bottle.

I knelt down beside her. She was totally out. I felt for a pulse and thought I could feel something. She was alive...but at my mercy. Here was the defining moment. An open goal for my killing career to get off the mark.

Rosie, this is for you!

I picked up my phone. "Could I order a taxi, please?"

She really should be in hospital. She shouldn't be lying in my bed, moaning in her sleep. What if she really did die? And what if she *didn't*? I couldn't keep a famous MP here, like Lawrence and Timmy. It would simply never work. Maybe it would be better for all concerned if she just passed away quietly in her sleep.

51. The hangover

Her head was hurting, her body was hurting. Her throat was dry – was that blood? There was a searing pain that seemed to run through her brain to every joint in her body. And there was something on her head – was she cut? She put her hand up to her head – *ouch*! *Jesus*, what had happened to her? There was something that didn't ...there was something deeply wrong.

Betsy opened her eyes. It hurt. She was not at home. She was lying in another bed, fully clothed. Her knees hurt, she realised, and there was a fierce pain in her right arm. There was a fierce pain everywhere. And there was a man. Next to her in the bed.

A much younger man. He was lying next to her and he was staring at her face.

Betsy sat bolt upright with a start and leapt back as he tried to reach for her. She tried to scream and promptly threw up over all over him.

"Sorry!" they both said in unison, as the young man leapt out of bed.

He sported a T-shirt and boxers and, she noticed, a hint of morning glory. It was something she hadn't seen in a few years, but somehow, the moment wasn't right.

"Who the hell are you?" she rasped, as the young man frantically turned his back on her and grabbed a pair of jeans from the floor. Her throat felt like it was broken when she spoke and she lay back on the pillow, feeling like she was going to be sick again.

The young man was pulling on his jeans and then removed his T-shirt, which was covered in her vomit.

"Sorry," he said again. "I'm Sean." He stood looking at her awkwardly and she looked back at him through her fingers. He looked vaguely familiar.

"You had an accident last night," he said. "You fell in the street and I brought you here as I couldn't afford a hospital for you. I'm sorry."

Betsy started as an image of the previous evening fleeted into her mind.

"*You*! The cat man!"

The image that had fleeted in seemed to dislodge parts of her brain and a fierce pain raked across her forehead again.

"Yes," he said. "Sorry. Would you – like a cup of tea?"

Betsy was aching, but unsettled enough by all this to struggle up and out of the bed. Her clothes were a mess. Her top was torn, her skirt was red with blood, which she noticed came from two deep cuts to her knees. And her head really hurt. She backed away from him as he approached, then sat down on the bed.

"Look, I'm not trying to hurt you," he said. "I brought you here to make sure you were ok."

Betsy put her head in her hands. "I think I need a doctor," she groaned.

"You probably do. Sorry, I didn't have the cash on me last night."

She didn't look up. "Dial 0208 241 9999. That's my doctor. Get her to come here. She has an agreement with the local hospitals and she'll get me in there if I need it."

All the effort of talking was too much and she lay back down on the bed. The young man hurried out of the room. A moment later, he walked back in – or she thought he did. But a different voice was speaking to her.

"I say, are you alright? You don't look too well."

She opened her eyes and peered up. A kindly looking old man was standing over her. She tried to shake her head, then realised it wasn't a good idea.

The young man had come back into the room. He stared at them both for a few moments, looking strangely afraid. Then he spoke. "I see you've met my grandad. What was that number again?"

The old man looked intently at them both. Then he chuckled.

"Your *grandad*? And I thought it was me who was losing my marbles!"

52. The mob

Lee Macken was relieved this meeting was taking place in one of the cavernous rooms at the Millennium Dome. There was no way this lot would all have fitted into his little office. Still, it was time he looked at upgrading his workspace – get something a bit more upmarket, away from the riff raff like Blondie and co.

There were over forty men in the room and they all looked like they meant business. Not poncy, wheeler dealer, pretend business - real, honest business. These were the new kids on the block – young, hungry, hard as nails. They were driven by two motives – profit and violence. Being able to marry the two together with the lucrative contracts Lee was now offering was a dream come true. These were men of the future: honest, hardworking, capitalist heroes. A far cry from Malone and his fucking wasters.

Lee had even got a small crew of them to do over Malone and the gang for breach of contract – they never had done that job in Lofting Road. Hopefully, Malone would learn a lesson and change his ways when he got out of hospital. Make that 'if' … with this lot working for him, he was at risk of stealing Keith Hartley's business more literally.

"Right!" Lee shouted to the brick shithouses gathered before him. "You all know why you're here! A certain Keith Hartley!"

A slight murmur went up at the mention of Hartley's name. These boys were scared of nobody, but if there was one person who just might perturb them a little bit, it was the one Lee had just mentioned.

Lee knew what the murmur meant.

"The man is a living legend. We all know that. A pioneer and one of the people who helped make Britain great again!"

Another murmur rose up. Whether it was appreciation or cynicism was hard to tell. Better cut to the chase.

"But he's a man who's had his day! A man who has taken to *anti-competitive practices* to try to save his own sorry arse! He's shown me fuckin'... *disrespect*!"

The mob cheered aggressively. Lee was starting to feel like a politician. Maybe one day...

"And what do we do to people who *disrespect* us?"

"Take 'em down!" yelled a brick shithouse at the back, to more cheers.

"That's right! That's fucking right, my friend!"

Now the shithouses were clapping and stamping. Lee held up his hand.

"Wait a minute. Hold on."

He relished the silence for a moment.

"I've heard some bad news. Mr Hartley has had a heart attack!"

"Aawwwwwwwwww!" pantomimed the shithouses.

"Yes. I'm afraid he's in hospital!"

"Awwwwwwwwwww!"

"It's touch and go!"

"Awwwwwwwwwww!"

"Well, all I can say is, let's hope the bastard survives! Because the minute he steps out of that hospital with its armed fucking guards on the wards…well, it won't be touch and go anymore, will it?"

"Noooooooo!" bellowed the shithouses.

"No. It'll be touch and fucking gone! We're gonna finish that spent old bastard once and for all!"

The shithouses were going crazy, like they were about to set off and do it now. He didn't want them all shot dead at the hospital, so he held up his hand again.

"And here's the good bit. For each and every one of you…I'm offering ten grand!"

A riotous cheer began, but Lee held up his hand again. Christ, this was enjoyable – maybe he should approach the People's Party and offer to modernise their approach – he could be a future Prime Minister!

"And should our friend Mr Hartley – who is *very* frail these days – somehow fail to survive this beating – well, I'll double that offer!"

Now they were positively baying and slapping one another on the back. Ok, he was bending the law. But if a man indulged in the perversity of anti-competitive practices, he got what was coming to him.

53. The confession

There was a long silence while the three of us gaped at each other. Me, the confused old man I was increasingly wishing I really had killed, and Britain's most left wing MP, who was sitting up in my bed. How the hell had my life come to this?

Eventually, I broke the silence.

"Sorry, Grandad, it's you who's confused. It's me. Sean." And I looked at the old duffer, pleadingly.

He had the fucking gall to smile back. "I know who you are. You're the young murderer chap. Sent to kill me but didn't have the heart!" And he beamed at Betsy, who was now struggling out of my bed.

"P-please, sit down!" I said to her. "He gets a bit confused sometimes."

Lawrence smiled again. "Well, I can't deny that. But I didn't know it was catching! I don't know why you're saying it, but you are absolutely not my grandson! I never had children, so that would be quite impossible. Though nice." And he smiled again, the fucking old *halfwit*!

I tried to smile at Betsy Saunders, but she was having none of it. She may be feeling rough, but she had suddenly developed a no-nonsense look and I realised I was in the presence of a cast iron bullshit detector.

"What's going on?" she said quietly.

"Would you like a cup of tea?" asked Lawrence, still smiling.

"No thanks, Lawrence," I sighed. "Could you just – leave us alone for a minute?"

He smiled and then winked. "Oh, certainly! I didn't mean to interfere!" And he shuffled off, humming to himself.

Betsy continued to appraise me coldly.

"It's a long story," I said.

"They all are," she said. "But to get to the point. Did you come to my house to kill me last night?"

I nodded and bit my lip, which was quivering a bit now. I was as rubbish a liar as I was a murderer.

"And this old chap? You were supposed to kill him too?"

"Yes."

"And that's how you make a living, is it? Killing people?"

"Well," I mumbled. "I don't seem to very good at it."

Tears were stinging my eyes. She looked at me for what seemed an age.

"So who do you work for?"

I shook my head. "Can't tell you that."

"Yes you can, Sean. I'm trying to help you here."

And now, for the first time, she looked at me with warmth and compassion. Someone else I'd set out to butcher to death was being kind to me. I burst into tears.

Betsy didn't hug me or do anything at all. She simply stood and watched, looking concerned. Waited for me to finish.

"It's Keith Hartley!" I blurted before the sobs had really gone, sounding like a boy whose balls had just dropped rather than been sentenced to removal.

"I see. So Keith Hartley was contracted to kill me?"

I nodded.

She seemed to hold her breath for a moment. "And do you know who by?"

I started to shake my head, but she was giving me that no nonsense look again.

"Bloke called Splash. Richard Splash?"

Her eyes seemed to gleam for a split second, then she nodded. "So tell me, Sean. How on earth did a nice boy like you end up working for a scumbag like Hartley?"

It was strange, but I felt a twinge at that, an urge to defend Keith. I realised with horror that I'd almost grown to *like* him.

"I sort of fell into it," I said. "Asked for a job as an apprentice. Thought it would be – you know. Glamorous."

She clearly didn't know. She looked utterly perplexed.

"He took me on. It was ok at first. Did a bit of PR, some work on his website, took some calls. It was when he wanted me to actually kill people that I started to realise it wasn't for me."

"But you stuck with it?"

"Bit too scared not to. He's not really a man you cross."

She frowned. "So you stayed on out of – fear of retribution?"

"Yes. I guess so. That and other stuff. I didn't want to let him down. Felt he'd trusted me. And he's a bit – well, mad, you know?"

"All the best business leaders are these days. But they don't all threaten to kill staff who decide to move on!"

"Well, he never did threaten that. Not explicitly, anyway. I just – well, I wasn't sure. And he's taken me on, you know? I didn't want to…"

"Let him down," she finished. "I'm afraid you're a terrible victim of our times, Sean. But I'd like to think I can help you."

"H-how?" I didn't say what I actually thought, which was that everyone knew she was the looniest MP in the country and her views on murder and similar trades were as antiquated as public services.

She clearly followed my line of thought anyway.

"You are a classic example of everything that is wrong with the world we live in," she announced, as I stood looking a bit sheepish. "But now that I can prove that a fellow MP tried to have me murdered, and that mass murderers like Hartley bully nice young men like you into working for them, maybe we'll begin to turn the corner!"

Oh Christ, she was obviously feeling better, she was spouting all that loony crap again. And suddenly I seemed to be involved in it.

54. Return of the cat killer

Rosie lay back in the bath and tried to shut out the noise. She was half asleep and had her earpod in, but she thought she heard shouting somewhere. Was that Sean? She sat up, shook the suds out of her hair and pulled out the earpod. Nothing. Maybe she'd dreamt it. Then she heard her front door slam.

"Sean?"

She hadn't given him a key. So who the fuck – it could only be…

The door was pushed open and Shirley - the cat-killing *cow* - stood on the threshold. Rosie started and tried to cover herself up.

"Shirley, what the f…?!"

Shirley appraised her coolly. "Don't be modest, Love. Been there, done that. Just came to return my key." She pulled a key out of her pocket and dropped it into the water.

In one movement, naked or not, Rosie was up and out of the bath, and clawing at her ex-girlfriends face.

"You fucking bitch!" she was screaming. "Fucking vicious, sick *cow*! *How could you do this to me?*"

Shirley was bigger and stronger, but was backing away under the furious onslaught. But she couldn't resist continuing to gloat.

"Don't take it so badly, Love. It was you dumped *me*, remember. Thought you might need a spare key!"

Then Rosie threw a right hook she didn't know she had. She didn't even know what a right hook *was*. But this one poleaxed Shirley.

Rosie was crying now, and shaking as she pulled a towel around herself. "You killed my fucking cat, you sick, vile BITCH!" she yelled. "And now I'm going to kill YOU!"

Shirley started to prop herself up on one arm, but a vicious clump from Rosie's right foot flattened her again. Rosie was beside herself with rage. She didn't know what she was doing anymore as she laid into Shirley, kicking her as she lay on the ground. There was blood coming from Shirley's nose. *Good*! Fucking BITCH! Shirley was trying to curl herself into a ball. There was a knocking on the front door, persistent. *Fuck* it! Shirley was doubling over now in pain, crying, terrified. Pathetic, murdering BITCH! Now someone was calling, calling her again and again.

"Rosie! Rosie! Look! I've found the cat!"

Rosie stopped suddenly. What was that? What the fuck? Had she *killed* Shirley? She bent down. No, but there was blood and there were broken teeth.

"Rosie?"

It was Sean's grandad. He'd obviously found his beloved Jimmy. Good for him. She couldn't let him in now, though, what would he think to find a half dead lesbian on her floor?

"Hello? Who's that?"

"It's Lawrence. Sean's grandfather. I've found Timmy."

"Jimmy."

"No, *Timmy*! Your cat! I think it may have been mine who was killed."

Rosie darted to the front door and opened it. Her heart leapt. It was *Timmy*! And he leapt too, out of the old man's arms and into her flat. Her eyes filled with tears.

"But I don't...what happened?!" she gulped.

The old man smiled with real happiness. "He just turned up outside. I knew it wasn't my cat. So I just called 'Timmy' and he trotted over."

"But...the night when...when Sean found the body, he brought me Timmy's collar. I don't understand!"

Now the old man looked a bit disturbed. "Ah," he said.

They stood like that for a few moments, each lost in their thoughts, Rosie cuddling Timmy like she'd never let him go and Timmy purring with delight. Then Lawrence's eyes widened as he stared over her shoulder.

Staggering down the hall was a woman who looked like she'd been in a fight with GBH Unlimited. Shirley was bleeding from her nose, had a huge bruise coming up under her eye and was staring with hatred – real, venomous hatred – at the cat in Rosie's arms.

She opened her mouth and spat out blood at Rosie's feet.

"I say," said Lawrence. "Are you quite well?"

"No she isn't," said Rosie. "This is the scheming cow who killed your cat! Except she was trying to kill mine!"

"Really?" said Lawrence. "Well, not to worry. Nine lives and all that."

Rosie looked at him in astonishment, but he continued.

"I've always valued human life above all others," he said. "And at the moment, you are my primary concern, young lady. You don't look well."

"Just fuck off!" spat Shirley. "I'm going to get to the bottom of this bollocks! I didn't pay Keith

Hartley a fucking fortune to bump off some other fucking cat!"

Rosie's stomach lurched. *"Keith Hartley?"*

Shirley was collecting herself now, but it was hard to remain smug as blood and tears trickled down her face.

"Yeah. Go to the best, I thought. Plus I knew that dork next door used to work for him – had a vague hope he might end up having to do it. But he didn't. And now I fucking *will*!"

And with a bellow of rage, she lurched at the cat and Timmy flew out of Rosie's arms. Shirley was raining punches down on Rosie's head now, and suddenly the fury had switched sides. Rosie was trying to grapple with her and could feel her towel slipping away. Lawrence was in the flat, trying to pull the mad bitch off, there were cries of rage from Shirley and desperate pleas from the old man. Then there was a thump, a shuddering, sickening sound, and the punches and kicks stopped. Rosie was curled up on the floor, naked and hurting. One of her ribs felt cracked. She opened her eyes.

Shirley was standing over her, dumbly, staring into the doorway. Lawrence was lying there, flat out, his mouth wide open. Blood was trickling from a gash in his head, which seemed to have hit her front door. And out of his ear. He had gone a pale blue colour.

"Oh, God! *What the fuck have you done to him, Shirley?*"

Shirley looked at Rosie again. There were tears of rage and fear in her eyes. Then she stepped over Rosie and Lawrence and bolted out into the hallway.

55. Rolling back the tide

This was the beginning of a genuinely new Britain, Betsy thought as she strolled confidently down the Mall. Her injuries and her hangover seemed to have dissipated, along with years of despair. Now, at long last, Splash and his ilk would be exposed for what they were – brutal fascist *bullies*!

She hadn't felt this powerful since she'd first been elected in Islington North and made that impassioned speech –she cringed when she thought of it now – about rolling back the tide of capitalism. Ok, she'd failed. But maybe if there were more people like Sean, able to speak up and talk about what 'New New Britain' really meant, the tide would finally start to turn.

Horace Ronson, Gregory Styles, Ryan Blake, they were all of the same ilk. Stupid, gutless politicians, none of them with any principles worth having. Well, if she was the only MP left who could tell it like it was, then she'd tell it like it was. She'd start her own revolution, here and now. When she got to the Kellogs House of Commons, she'd put down a motion for an emergency debate. If they refused, she'd come outside and tell the cameras exactly what she had been going to tell the House.

Which was…that Richard Splash had contracted Keith Hartley to kill her. That Hartley's employee had been unable to carry out his orders and was only working for Hartley because he was scared of him. That…didn't add up to a case that would roll back any tides.

Her stride slowed to a snail's pace as the wind left her sails. Maybe she was hung over, after all. She stopped still by Horse Guard's Parade.

What had she been thinking? What had propelled her all this way from Sean's flat – despite his desperate protestations that she'd be signing both their death warrants – to the Kellogs Commons, to once again try to start a one-woman revolution? Anger? Fear? Delusion?

Oh sure, it would ruffle a few feathers in the Westminster village. Splash would be arrested, maybe imprisoned if the case could be proved – but a quaking Sean wouldn't be the most reliable witness. But what had ever made her think that the whole of New New Britain would come tumbling down on the back of an attempt to kill a loony leftie MP and a sob story from a lad not up to doing his job? It was almost more likely that they'd make a new case for MPs having the same rights as anyone else to kill people.

Her eyes filled with tears as she stared at the Mother of all Parliaments. When she thought of the history of this place, the fight for universal suffrage, the impassioned debates, the great speeches…and what had become of it? It was nothing but a half-hearted, ineffective, commercially-sponsored regulator of an increasingly insane market.

A scruffy looking man was stumbling towards her. She went to put her hand in her pocket. The only way to help the homeless was to give them what you could so they could live another day. She remembered her father saying there used to be organisations for people like these and governments used to try to find houses for them to live in. It sounded somewhat quaint now. The man was smiling as he walked towards her and she smiled back… then saw the revolver in his hand.

She had no time to scream. There was a loud crack and her world shattered into tiny fragments.

56. Chaos at the hospital

I had to find Keith. I had to get to him first.

I knew he was a dangerous man, I knew he would be livid and I knew he might kill me. But he couldn't do that strapped up in a hospital bed. Maybe I could reason with him, warn him of what Betsy Saunders was about to do. Apologise. I didn't know what I was going to say. But I had to find him before someone else did – Betsy, Archie, Police UK, the press…

I sat in the back of the taxi, my mind a whirl. Lawrence had looked so upset when I'd bawled him out, but what did the crazy old fool expect? He'd blown our cover now, good and proper. When he'd heard me arguing with Betsy in the hallway, he seemed to have switched back on again. *Too fucking late*, pal! When I'd walked back into the living room, his eyes were full of tears.

"I've really done it this time, haven't I?"

"Yes you fucking well HAVE! You stupid, stupid, *senile* old man! You've *really done it this time* alright! Except it's not about forgetting the name of a cat or that your wife is a murderous gold-digger! It's getting me fucking KILLED! Thank you so fucking *much*!"

And I'd stormed around the flat, throwing things, panic in my soul as my life fell to bits around me. What to do? Run next door and confess all to Rosie? Tell her that I loved her more than anything, but she probably wouldn't see me again?

That it was all my fault for not bumping off this crazy old twat who wasn't even my grandad, oh and her cat wasn't dead, that was me too and Lord, what a fucking *mess*!!!

Lawrence just sat there looking wretched while I ranted and raved and panicked and eventually decided that I had to get to Keith first, Keith sort of liked me, maybe he'd be reasonable. It was a faint hope. Britain's most notorious murderer in surprise act of benevolence towards employee who fucks over his business. I knew it was a non-existent fantasy. But everything was jangling now, the truth was forcing its way to the surface and it was like it couldn't be stopped. If I survived Keith, it was Rosie next. If he didn't kill me, the moment of truth with her surely would.

"Homerton Hospital, Mate?"

I hadn't realised that we were standing still. The taxi had pulled up outside. Ahead of me, I could see a crew of Ambient Ambulance staff rushing in someone on a stretcher. There were Police UK people there too, must be a suspect one. Or somebody famous.

"Do you want this hospital or not, mate? Time's money, y'know."

"Sorry," I said absently. I paid and got out, staring up at the hospital entrance. Someone had said to me once that in years gone by, most lives started and ended in hospitals. There was no way the country could afford it, of course, but it had a nice symmetry. And my own life was about to end in hospital – or at least sentence would be passed here. I took a deep breath and stepped inside.

Inside the hospital was absolute chaos. There were TV cameras, reporters talking frantically into their phones, Police UK staff and over in the corner, talking to a TV camera, it looked like Gregory Styles, the Leader of the Opposition. Something pretty huge had gone off. I didn't really care what. Then it hit me.

Had she already done it? Had Betsy been quicker than I thought? She'd insisted she was going to 'raise it in the House of Commons', as that was only proper or some such crap, and I'd thought that had bought me a bit of time. Maybe she'd phoned ahead? Maybe they do all their debates and stuff by text these days? I don't really follow any of that bollocks.

I inched closer towards Gregory Styles, but a young woman in a sharp suit cut across me.

"Stand back, please," she said.

I moved away, gaping at the scene ahead of me. Then I spotted a red head walking towards me.

"Miranda!"

She nodded curtly. She clearly hadn't forgotten our last meeting.

"What's happened?" I asked. I felt strangely breathless.

"Like I'd tell you." She turned away towards the throng.

"Look," I croaked. "I'm sorry. I'm really, really sorry. For everything."

Miranda turned and looked at me.

"What's wrong, Sean?"

There was concern in her eyes. And if Miranda was concerned, I must have looked twice as bad as I felt.

"Nothing. I just...tell me what's going on!"

Miranda looked at me strangely, as if trying to work something out. Then she looked over her shoulder, then back at me.

"MP's been shot. Betsy something or other."

"Saunders?"

"That's it. See you."

And she turned and hurried away.

I stood gawping after her. I should have been jumping for joy. My stomach wouldn't let me. All I could think was that a decent, caring person – who had tried really hard in her own way to help me – had come to a horrible end. Poor, poor Betsy.

Then I heard a reporter next to me gabbling into his phone. "She's still alive, apparently. No-one knows yet, but seems it might not be fatal!"

Sentence had merely been deferred. But so had my desire to confess all to Keith. My heart jumped in my chest and I rushed back out the front door.

The cab was still waiting and the cabbie scowled slightly. "Changed your mind again?"

"Losing it entirely," I said, swinging my legs into the back seat. I wasn't joking, either.

57. Death in the doorway

Tears streaked Rosie's face as she sat cradling Lawrence in her arms. She knew the old man was dying. She'd tried to call am ambulance, but she couldn't get one anywhere. She'd tried to call Sean, but his phone was off. In the end, she'd found a number for Sara on her phone and tried ringing it, but to no avail. Probably lost in the flood.

Lawrence's breathing came in rasps now. She kissed the old man on his forehead and started as he opened his eyes.

"Ah, Rosie", he said.

She stroked his face.

"Forgive him…" he wheezed. "He meant no bad."

"Forgive Shirley?"

"Sean," he said. "He loves you so much."

She stroked his head again. He made no sense. Then her phone rang. She picked it up and saw Sara's face, glowering at her.

"Sara!"

"What do you want? Where's Sean? I've nowhere to sleep tonight and I…what's wrong?"

"Sara, look, I've got bad news. Your grandad. He's had a very bad fall and…"

"I don't have a grandad."

"You do! Sean tracked him down! Lawrence?" And she swung around the phone, so Sara could see the old man's face, then hastily swung it back again.

Sara wrinkled her nose. "I don't know him. Both my grandads died when I was young and neither of them was called Lawrence. Is that guy ok?"

Rosie looked at the old man again, mystified. He smiled softly and closed his eyes again.

"So…who is this guy? Sean told me he was…" She stopped and ran her fingers through her hair. "Sara, did either of your grandfathers have a cat? One that looked like mine?"

Sara looked at her as if she was crazy. "Look, shouldn't you be getting help or something?"

Lawrence suddenly wheezed again and lurched forward, opening his eyes. Then he lay still, his eyes wide open and staring. Rosie screamed.

"*Oh my God*, Sara! Oh my *God*!"

"What? Has he…?"

Rosie was sobbing now, as she reached across and closed Lawrence's eyes for the last time.

"I'm just over in Euston," Sara said. "I'll get a cab and be with you in ten!"

Rosie cradled the old man again, sobbing and bewildered. If this man wasn't Sean's grandfather, why had he told her he was? How had Sean had Timmy's collar when Timmy was still alive? And - *fucking hell, Shirley had just killed a sweet old man!* She picked up her phone again – she had a number somewhere for Police UK.

As she did so, the outside door from the street burst open and two men in Police UK uniforms stood there. Well, that was service. They took in the scene at a glance – the open front door, the old man lying in the arms of the naked young female. *Christ, she was naked!* Rosie leapt up and was mortified to recognise one of the two men was Will, Miranda's new squeeze.

"One minute!" she garbled, reaching for her towel.

"We had reports of a commotion," Will said. "I guess that was here?"

Rosie pulled the towel around herself and burst into tears again.

58. The condemned man

Park benches. They say that in the soap operas and films of years gone by, they had an iconic meaning. Someone sitting alone on a park bench wasn't enjoying the sunshine, idling away the day or waiting for someone else. No, being on a park bench meant your life was starting to crumple around you. And that's just how I felt now, sitting in the park, staring into the distance at nothing in particular.

I'd paced around the block several times, but I couldn't summon up the courage to go in and face Rosie. The truth was outing itself and sooner or later, she was going to know the facts. Betsy Saunders would recover and then my image would be emblazoned across every TV in the country – probably while my actual body was face down in the Thames.

How much could I tell her? The whole truth – or just bits of it? No, once she found out Lawrence was not my grandfather, it wouldn't take her long to work out that Timmy's disappearance had been my work too. If she could forgive my other lies, I knew she would never forgive me that. I'd got the girl of my dreams against all the odds and I had blown it in the most spectacular fashion imaginable. All I wanted now was the chance to put my side, to apologise, to tell her I loved her so much it ached. And to say goodbye.

I tried to tell myself it didn't really matter if Rosie dumped me. I wasn't going to be alive much longer anyway. What if she forgave everything?

With her love and support, her understanding, Christ, I'd go to Keith and tell him exactly what I thought of his sick profession and that he could stick his job up his fat arse! Well no, I wouldn't, but you get the picture. At least if Rosie still loved me, I'd feel I had something to live for.

What tore me apart was the thought of her sitting in her flat now, blissfully unaware of everything. Oh, I knew Rosie had had her doubts in the beginning – great, looming ones that cast shadows over everything at times. But I also knew she'd turned the corner, she'd fallen for me as more than a friend. Rosie had fallen in love with me. That was a miracle and it was going to end up being the biggest and most important achievement of my life.

Keith wouldn't stay in hospital long. Once he knew what had happened with Betsy, he'd be itching to get out of there and deal with me. I knew the score really. The man had no room for sentiment and I'd let him down badly, maybe even destroyed his business and sent him back to prison.

How many times had I asked myself the question: *why?* Walking into his shop that day was the biggest mistake I ever made. Sure, we all want to work in these funky new industries, but what had made me ever think that I could become a hired killer? Miranda was right – I couldn't hurt a fly. I'd hurt her, though - I realised that now, and maybe she'd hurt me too – we were both too in love with other people to make things work, but it had been much better than I'd ever admitted. She wasn't Rosie, I wasn't Will, but we'd had good times together. I wished I'd been able to make my peace with her, but I guessed there was still too much resentment on either side.

And Sara. I'd have to call her – I didn't want to go to my death with the last words between us being cross ones, even if that wasn't untypical of our relationship over the years. I didn't even want to think about Mum and Dad. Dad would probably agree with Betsy Saunders that I was a victim of the times. It was hard to imagine that Mum wouldn't laugh, just a little bit, once she was over the shock and the pain of losing me.

I'm too young to die, I thought. Too young to leave all these people behind. But without Rosie, what is there to live for? Facing her first, getting it over with, will make the final showdown with Keith easier.

I got up from the bench. Adrenalin and emotion coursed through my veins. Five minutes up the road was my flat - and Rosie's. I was five minutes away from the worst moments of my life.

59. The creditor

Splash stared glumly at the plasma screen. The champagne cork he'd popped sat almost embarrassed on the floor, the steam still rising from the untouched bottle on the coffee table. He thought he'd got a real pro in to take out that socialist whore. But now the reports were saying that she'd survived. Betsy Saunders was still alive and Keith Hartley, Britain's number one murderer, had buggered things up.

He was surprised to hear the doorbell ring. Splash received few visitors these days. He got up to answer it, then decided against. It might be more of those insolent Police UK types, asking questions about the attempt on Betsy Saunders' life. They'd never make it stick to him, but he wasn't up for more insolence right now.

Gregory Styles was on the TV, calling for a 'full and proper investigation'. Pompous ass. British American Heroin were clearly lobbying to run the inquiry - their MD, Howard Clarke, was on puffing joints and waxing lyrical about freedom of speech applying even to extremists.

The doorbell kept ringing and ringing and now someone was banging on the window. For Christ's sake! Splash went out into the hallway and opened the door. Standing before him, with a stupid grin on his face, was the scruffy figure of Niall Burke.

Splash glared at him. "What on *earth* are you doing here?"

Burke grinned again. "Job done. Come for my cash."

"What are you talking about? I told you never to come here!"

"Well, I thought you might want to shake the hand that shot Betsy dead!"

Couldn't this goon keep his voice down? Reluctantly, Splash ushered him inside.

"Wight! What are you talking about, Burke?"

Burke smiled. "You haven't heard? I done for Betsy Saunders. Reconsidered your offer, innit? She's a goner."

Splash angrily took Burke by the arm and guided him into his living room. The very thought that such a disgusting man should enter his living area appalled him.

"See you got the champers out to celebrate!"

"On the contwawy, I'm not celebwating anything. According to the latest weports, Betsy Saunders survived. Nor do I wecall weaching any agweement with you over this matter. I had in fact contwacted someone else – now I know you were involved, I begin to see what's gone wrong!"

Burke looked suddenly incensed. "Oy, hold up! I want my money!"

"Money for what? You haven't even killed her!"

"I did! I saw her die!"

"You saw her fall over, Burke! It's not quite the same thing!"

Burke looked a bit crestfallen. "I'm not great with guns. But you have my word I'll finish her off, innit?"

"It's a bit late for that now! She's going to be protected day and night, there will be an inquiwy, fingers will be pointed at me – not least hers, because, thanks to you, she is still alive! Had you let Keith Hartley get on with the job…"

"Hartley! You are goin' upmarket! Anyway, he's at death's door, innit?"

"What?"

"Keith Hartley. Had a heart attack, innit? He's in Homerton Hospital."

"He's *what*? Nobody told me!"

"Yeah. Straight up."

Splash stared at the plasma screen, which still had the same headline: MP SHOT - LIVE FROM HOMERTON HOSPITAL.

"I wonder…," he said.

60. Waking up lucky

Images swam in Betsy's mind. Half-formed images on a cloudy purple background. Ryan Blake and his oily smile, Sean with his tears and his hopeless lies, the sweet old man who wasn't really his grandfather, Richard Splash's leering face. The gun. *Oh God, the gun…*

She felt no pain. She could remember only the scruffy man, the gun and the loud bang. Maybe this was what happened after you died. Just bits of memories, floating around on a purple sea. Splash had won. He'd had her shot dead, silenced her forever. And at that thought, anger welled inside her, anger that was all too alive, all too real. *She wasn't dead.* She was waking up.

She flicked open her eyes. It felt like an effort. She was lying in bed. For the second time in 24 hours, she had woken up to find a young man staring at her. This one sat on a chair opposite her bed, in a white coat. And he was *gorgeous.*

"Hello! We've been waiting for you to wake up!"

She put her hand to her head. She could feel a bandage there, but still no pain. They'd obviously put her on painkillers.

"You're on a morphine drip and you've been fitted with a catheter," the young man explained. "Try not to move about too much, you've had a nasty experience."

"Nasty?" She was almost surprised to find that her voice worked. "I've been shot!"

"I know," he said. "And you need to get to some rest!

She put her hand to her head again. "I don't understand why I'm not dead?"

He smiled and his green eyes danced. Gosh, he was gorgeous. Probably gay. "The bloke was a bad shot. The bullet only grazed the side of your head. Enough to knock you out and you're probably concussed from the fall, but other than that…you're very lucky."

She smiled back. "People rarely say that to me. The man *was* at point blank range, though."

"So you remember everything?"

"Very much so. I remember being shot and I know who set it up. I'd be keen to talk to whichever policing firm is investigating."

"Police UK. They're waiting outside, but I've told them not just now. You need to rest."

"No listen, Doctor…?"

"Doctor Crossley. Mike."

"Listen, Mike. What I have to say to them is important. Can you send them in now?"

He frowned. "I really shouldn't. But if you're sure?"

She nodded and yawned. Gosh, he really was gorgeous. Almost certainly gay. She closed her eyes again and found herself back in the purple sea.

61. Breaking Rosie's heart

All in all, this was not an encouraging start. I knocked on Rosie's door and she let me in without a word. She led me through to the living room, where I was shocked to see Sara sitting on the sofa. And sitting on Sara's knee, purring his little heart out, was *Timmy*. Rosie sat down next to Sara and gestured to the chair opposite without a word. I sat.

Rosie looked at me. "Lawrence is dead," she said flatly.

I leapt up immediately, my guts churning. "What?! He's *what*? He – how?"

She looked at me levelly. "Shirley came back. We got in a fight, he tried to break it up. She hit him, he fell and hit his head on the door. He's dead."

I bowed my head. I couldn't take it in. That Lawrence should survive Saskia's conspiracy and his own tendency to drop us in the shit and die such a bizarre death. I couldn't believe it. And then I remembered how I'd torn into him when we last spoke. I felt like I'd been kicked in the stomach.

Sara put Timmy down and came across and put her hand on my arm. She didn't have the same accusing air about her as Rosie did, but it was clear that she too was awaiting some sort of explanation.

"Come on, Timmy," Rosie said as he climbed up on to her lap and I knew then the game was up.

"I looked up at her. "I'm sorry," I said. "So truly sorry."

Her expression didn't change. "For what?"

I took a deep breath. "I've been really stupid. I've lied to you. To both of you. And to me, actually."

Sara took her hand from my arm now, but sat on the arm of the chair, watching me. Rosie stayed silent.

"I think you know some of it?" I said.

Rosie looked at me. Now I could see real pain in her eyes. "Well, I know Timmy isn't dead and I know Lawrence wasn't your grandfather. Is there more?"

"I...didn't do any of this on purpose..."

"What? Tell me my cat was dead? That somebody cut his *throat*? *Bring me his fucking collar*? Convince a poorly old man to play along with it? *Do you realise just how fucking sick that is?*"

Tears were starting to roll down her face now, tears of rage. And her voice was rising.

"I really, really can't believe you would do this to me! To anybody! But that's you, isn't it? You just wanted to control me, keep me sweet, make me believe it could all work out with you – I thought fucking Shirley was a headcase, but you, you're out on your own! You want fucking locking up!"

I didn't know what to say. I just sat and stared at her as she screamed at me. The reality felt much, much worse than the fear of it had – it's meant to work the other way around. I'd broken the most precious thing I'd ever owned: Rosie's heart.

"Say something, Sean," Sara said. "Tell us what happened – I know you're not a bad person..."

"Yes, say something, Sean!" spat Rosie. "I'd love to fucking hear it!"

So I did. I told them the whole story. How I'd got the job with Keith, then realised just how gruesome and horrific it was, but been too terrified of him and too set on making myself more interesting to quit. How I'd got in deeper and then the contract had come in for Timmy (cue more tears of fury from Rosie). Then I told them about Lawrence and our agreement and even though I knew it sounded insane, about my desperate attempts to cover for him losing Timmy with the grandad story. I told them about the body in the fridge, about Keith's heart attack, about Archie's threats against the two of them, about Betsy Saunders and her plan to publicise the whole story. At this point, Sara put her hand on my arm again, looking alarmed.

"Please tell me it wasn't you who shot her today?"

I shook my head. "I don't know anything about that," I said. "All I know is that I will die soon. Keith will kill me when he finds out, without a doubt. I just wanted to say, Rosie, that I do love you, with all my heart. Not wanting to lose you stopped me running away weeks ago. I wish I hadn't tried to be something I'm not and I wish I hadn't lied to you. I really wish I hadn't hurt you like I did over Timmy. And I know, I *know* I've got everything wrong. I just want to say - and I want you to remember - that I'm really sorry."

Sara was crying now as well, tears streaking down her face. I felt numb. Rosie sat on her sofa, stroking Timmy, looking strangely calm.

"I wish," she said. "I really wish, that you were able to love me enough to tell me all this before it got so out of hand. I wish you'd loved me enough not to break my heart over Timmy. And I wish you'd loved me enough not to break it again now."

She looked at me when she said that and it was a look not of anger, but burning regret. The pain in her eyes was tearing a hole in my heart. The numbness had gone now. I felt physically sick.

"Rosie, I love you more than anything else in the world. Loving you has been the only thing that's kept me going."

She shook her head. "But you didn't love me *enough*," she said. "That's what really happened, Sean. When you love someone, you want to share things with them."

"I thought I'd lose you…"

"And you did," she finished. "But not because I didn't love *you* enough. Because you didn't love *me* enough."

To hear that, after all I'd been through. The angst of my life since I'd met her, the madness since Keith had taken me on – she was all that had mattered, through it all. And now I would go to meet my nemesis knowing that she thought we had imploded because I didn't love her *enough*. It was viciously unfair.

"But Archie said he'd…"

She shook her head. It was over.

I stood up. "Well," I said, gulping back tears. "It's quite likely that you won't see me again."

Rosie said nothing, she just sat stroking Timmy, a tear trickling down her face and on to her chin.

"Rosie?" said Sara. "Have you nothing to say to Sean?"

"One thing," Rosie said. "I really did love you, Sean. But if you die now, it won't matter. Because the Sean I knew is dead already."

And that was that. The Sean I knew being pretty much dead as well, I got up and walked back across the hallway into my own flat. I heard Sara shouting and slamming Rosie's door, then the outside door. And I sat on the kitchen floor, crying my heart out.

62. A few home truths

Betsy woke with a sudden jolt. It was night time. Where were the Police UK bods? She must have fallen asleep. That wouldn't do – she had to get the truth out there as soon as possible. Sean's life might depend on it – and so might hers. She reached for the bedside remote and turned on the light.

It was nearly midnight. They'd taken the drip and the catheter off. Good. Meant she could stretch her legs and go to the loo. She swung her legs out of bed and then walked out into the corridor. An armed guard sat outside the room – snoozing. Charming…it was so good to know she was protected! There was another ward to the left, marked 'Cardiology', and a couple of private wards like her own opposite. The toilets must be down the corridor to the right. She was about to set off, when she noticed something that made her start.

The ward opposite had a name tag on the door: K.HARTLEY. *Under care of Doctor R Barnes, Cardiologist. Supported by Coca Cola and Nike.* Keith Hartley, she knew now for certain, was the man in her garden with the knife the other night. The man who had seemingly had a heart attack. Surely this must be the same man? The temptation was too great. She crept across the corridor, pushed open the door and looked in.

A man lay on the bed, connected to a heart monitor, snoring. He was facing away from her, but the bulk and the grey hair made her pretty sure. She closed the door quietly behind her and walked nearer. Then the man woke with a sudden start, pressed his remote and turned on the lights.

Now she recognised him. And he recognised *her*. He gave a weird grimace of acknowledgement. She backed away.

"You tried to kill me!" she said.

He stretched and rubbed his eyes. "No offence meant. Just bisniss."

"Illegal business! Killing an MP is against the law."

He shrugged as he sat up in bed. Betsy backed away further. "One move from you and I'll scream!"

"You think I'd bump you off 'ere, in t'middle of an 'ospital! I'd be prime suspect! I'm not daft, ya know!"

"Well, if I were you, I'd be thinking seriously about it."

"Well you're not me. An' I've yet to see you think seriously about anything. Whingin' PC cow! Now goodnight."

"You don't know what I know, then."

"Stop talkin' in fookin' riddles, woman cut to t'chase!!"

"You'd better start listening" she quivered. "Because I know exactly what's been going on and I'm going to finish you once and for all!"

Hartley chortled at that. "Behave, woman! Doctor Barnes told me you got shot. It were my lad. Sorry about that. Fookin' shootin' is bad enough, but the puff seems to 'ave missed! Like to see you prove it were us, though."

"Oh, I can," she said. "You'd better listen to me, because I'm about to tell you a few home truths!"

Keith chuckled again, with less conviction, but sat up further in the bed.

"It wasn't 'your lad' who shot me. It was someone else. 'Your lad' took me to his flat, put me up for the night and broke down in tears at the thought of killing me. And not just me. He has an old man living in his flat – Lawrence Fry – who has been there since Sean was meant to murder him and burn the body. And his girlfriend's cat's been living there too – another one you tried to force him to kill. And the only reason he's carried on working for you is because he's terrified that if he leaves, you'll murder *him*! Is that the behaviour of a civilised employer?!"

Keith stared at her throughout this outburst. Then suddenly, his eyes blazed.

"That fookin' little dweeb!" he muttered. "I'll kill 'im!"

"Oh, really?" Betsy went on, the pitch of her voice rising with her anger. "Like you were going to kill me? I don't think so! You're finished, you despicable old bastard! Finished!"

Now Keith leapt forward in the bed, sending the monitor into a frenzy of beeps. Betsy hurriedly backed out into the corridor and closed the door, then immediately heard a mighty crash. So did the sleeping security guard.

"Hey! What's going on?"

The door to Hartley's room burst open and there he was on the threshold, glowering at her, pulling electrodes and wires off himself. The machine was on the floor, still beeping.

The guard drew his gun.

"Look, Mr Hartley, we don't want any trouble…"

Keith looked from the guard, to Betsy, to the gun, as though making a calculation. Then suddenly, he shook his enormous head from side to side.

"Bad dream," he said. "Could you get someone to come and fix things up again?"

The guard nodded and picked up his radio. Still Keith stood in the doorway, hovering. Betsy backed away slightly. Then he nodded at her, his eyes boring into hers, and closed the door from the inside.

63. Keith's list

For God's sake, it was only 7am! Who on earth could be ringing at this time? If it was that bloody little pleb Niall Burke...

Splash sat up in his bed. The all-night porn channel he'd gone to sleep to was still flickering and his phone was still ringing. This was the third call.

He picked it up and was amazed to see a pyjama-clad Keith Hartley staring back. Hartley looked like he was outside - what the hell was going on?

"Mr Hartley. Stwange time to call?"

Hartley looked apoplectic. "Strange time to fookin' call! What the fook are you doin', payin' some amateur to fook up the Saunders job!"

"I did not!"

"Yes ya fookin' did! An' now I'm in deep shite!"

"Mr Hartley, I'll thank you not to use that tone with me! I paid nobody – and indeed, your company hasn't delivered on your pwomise to kill her! You've had plenty of time now..."

"Listen, Splash, you talk to me like that again, you're a dead man. Now tell me what 'appened!"

Splash gulped. "Ok...a man who has done some work with me in the past knew of my plans and twied to cawy them out. Without my authowisation!"

"So it were one of your boys, then. As I fookin' thought! You *twat*!""

Splash couldn't help but be riled by the man's insolence. "Look, I've asked you once not to speak to me like that! You have a bad attitude! It was your company that botched things! Overwated, it seems!"

Hartley didn't answer and Splash looked again at his phone. Hartley's eyes were on fire. He suddenly looked every inch the Keith Hartley of legend. A huge, terrifying man, who now looked to be driven by an all-consuming fury. And he was definitely out of doors in those pyjamas.

"Where are you? I – er – thought you were in Homerton? You could have kil..."

"I'm out. Discharged meself. I've a few scores to settle and you've just added to 'em, Dick Splash! Say yer goodbyes. You're on my fookin' list!"

Splash dropped the phone. When he picked it up again, Keith Hartley had rung off.

Splash got back into bed and hid under the covers. Then, still cringing, he reached for his phone again and called Burke.

"Ah N-Niall," he said. "Stwange time to call, I know. But it's an emergency! I'll double your money if you help me out. I'll twiple it! *Please*...?"

64. Showdown

There was something knocking on my mind, Something persistent, trying to tell me – what? Something bad. I was waking up. Then it hit me. The previous day. The sickening, soul-destroying, previous day. I was lying on the sofa, fully clothed. And my life was over. And my phone was ringing, incessantly.

I reached into my pocket and picked it up. It was Sara, crying hysterically, terrified.

What the fuck?

"Sara! Where are you?"

Now another face appeared on the phone. A big, miserable face, in spite of its sardonic grin.

Archie.

"Archie! What the fuck's going on!"

"Well. This little minx 'as spent the night wi' Uncle Archie! 'Aven't you, Darlin?"

"You fucking…if you've touched one hair of her head…"

Archie tried to arch an eyebrow. "Got me scared now. She put Keith's windows through yesterday an' I caught her. Kept 'er under lock and key till I could speak to 'im." His tone hardened. "'E wants you down 'ere. Sharpish."

I was already up and pulling my shoes on. "You kept her there all night! You fucking …"

"Steady, Lad. Stop swearin'. You don't want to meet yer maker on bad terms!"

"Sean!" Sara shouted. "Don't come! Keith knows everything!"

Archie nodded. "'E does too. Knows I were reight all along about you. So mebbe *don't* come. But bear in mind that if Keith gets 'ere before you do, yer sister gets 'er throat cut. Think on."

And he hung up.

Jesus Christ, Sara, what have I done to you! Why didn't I even think about where she'd gone yesterday? I had to get there, had to get there before Keith! And I just *knew* he would kill me. But I'd known that already. Now it was about stopping him killing Sara as well. The stupid, impulsive, feisty little cow!

I honestly thought about knocking on Rosie's door, telling her what had happened, asking for her support – but what could she do? I thought about calling Police UK – but finding someone being killed in a murderer's shop was hardly a crime! I ran out of the flat and pelted down the street, hailed the first cab I saw even though it's walking distance, and was there in a matter of minutes.

A surreal scene greeted me. The front window was completely trashed and bits of glass were everywhere, inside and out. Archie sat behind the desk, reading the paper. Sara – poor little Sara! – was tied by thick ropes to a table in the middle of the room. What any casual visitor or passer-by was to make of this, I don't know. But Archie didn't care.

"Reight," he greeted me. "Sit down and shurrup."

"No! Not until you untie her!"

"Don't push your luck. You're not in a position to bargain. If you want 'er to gerrout of 'ere alive, shut yer gob!"

I bent down to Sara and hugged her. She was too tightly bound to hug back, but wept hysterically again.

"Archie, these ropes are too tight! You'll give her gangrene!"

"I won't tell you again, Lad! Shut it!"

So we sat in silence, broken only by the rustle of Archie's paper and Sara's tiny sobs. The shop seemed to smell more of grease than ever today. *I had to make sure I got Sara out of here alive*. It would be the last thing I did, but I had to do it. I'd thought my heart couldn't ache any more, but seeing my little sister bound up, hearing her sobs and knowing she'd got into all of this because of me, was just breaking it all over again.

She had looked at me yesterday with such compassion – me, who'd dissed her friends after their near-death experience and let her walk off out of my life just after she'd nearly drowned. And here she was, tied up and prepared for execution, for being angry and brave and stupid enough to put a psychopath's windows through on my behalf…so who was the self-centred one here? I had to somehow persuade Keith to let her go first – I couldn't die not knowing whether she would live. Oh *God, Mum and Dad…!*

The door to the shop opened. The nemesis moment I'd probably been heading towards when I first entered this smelly old shop had arrived.

Or had it? I stood up, turned around, and found myself facing Will and Miranda. They surveyed the scene ahead of them in some bewilderment.

"What's going on, Sean?" Miranda asked. "What are you doing to Sara?"

Archie stepped out from behind the desk. "It's bisniss. No concern o' yours."

"Well, it just might be!" stormed Miranda. "Sean – she's your sister, for Christ's sake! I know you have strange views about families, but…"

Will held up his hand officiously. "We'll come to all that in a minute. My first duty here is to establish the whereabouts of Mr Hartley?"

"That's me," sneered Archie.

"Mr *Keith* Hartley. We are here to question him – *and* his associates – about the attempted illegal murder of Betsy Saunders and the fraudulent death of Mr Lawrence Fry. We would like to ask…"
BANG!

In a flash, the door had opened and Will had been floored by a rabbit punch to the back of the neck. This time, my nemesis really had arrived – bizarrely clad in a pair of stripy pyjamas. Miranda pulled out her radio, but Archie grabbed her by the throat and forced it from her hand. Then Keith punched her brutally in the stomach.

"Oy!" I yelled. "There's no need for that!"

Miranda collapsed to the floor, winded. "Tie 'er up, Archie," said Keith. Then, as Archie busied himself pulling out a dirty piece of rope from under the counter, Keith looked at me for the first time.

"So," he said.

"So," I said back.

He shook his big head at me as Archie dragged Miranda along the floor, in spite of her furious protests.

"You've let me down, Shawn," he said.

"I know. And I know what that means. But first you have to let these two go."

"No," he said. "I've scores to settle wi' all of 'em."

My heart sank into hell and my voice shook with emotion. "Brave man, aren't you? Killing women?!"

"Don't talk to me about balls, Shawn. You've got none. An' look at my shop. You seriously think I'd let some little slapper get away wi' this?"

"She was sticking up for me!"

"Aye - I made that mistake meself once! No, you've all played yer part. These two clowns wi' their stupid rules and regulations. Your sister smashin' my shop. But you – I never would 'ave thought it. You've brought me down, Lad."

"I didn't mean to! I was trying to help!"

"I thought you 'ad the madness. I really thought ya did! Well, it just shows how wrong you can be."

"You're the one who's fucking mad!" Sara suddenly bellowed.

"Aye, Lass," he said. "Mad to take on this little squirt! More trouble than I ever thought. Never seriously thought I'd end up killin' 'im."

He sighed, walked behind the counter and opened the drawer. I knew what was in there. Keith's carving knives. There was no point in running – he'd only kill the others if I did. Miranda was now tied up to the same table as Sara. And Will lay unconscious on the floor, drained of all pomposity.

"Listen, Keith," I said breathlessly. "You can't do this! Ok, kill me if you want to – but you can't go around murdering police officers and vandals!"

"I can murder 'oo I want, Shawn. An' I will."

Now he was walking towards me. It seemed pointless going down without a fight. I drew back my hand and punched him squarely on the nose, as hard as I could. Keith was so stunned that he almost dropped the knife, but the blow didn't move him an inch.

Archie laughed aloud. "Watch out, Keith! 'E's an apprentice mur-derer, you know!"

Keith didn't say anything. His face was uncomfortably close to mine now and he just stared at me, the carving knife still in his hand.

"Oh, aye. An *apprentice*. That were your idea, weren't it, Shawn? I took you on, trained you up, took you in to my bisniss, even my 'ouse. An' you repaid me wi' lies and then squealed on me. Why?"

"Just fuckin' do it, Keith!" Archie shouted.

"No! Please, no!" Sara was sobbing.

"Please don't!" wailed Miranda.

Keith said nothing in response. He just carried on staring at me..

"Why, Shawn?" he asked me again.

Suddenly, there was a huge commotion outside. A number of cars screeched to a halt and all at once there seemed to be people everywhere, running and shouting. Then the door burst open and twenty or thirty huge men stood on the threshold. One of them pushed his way to the front.

"Morning all. Lee Macken, GBH Unlimited. This is a takeover bid – an aggressive one!"

Keith kept the carving knife in his hand and pushed me aside as the mob rushed forward. I flew across the room, crashing into the table where Sara and Miranda were tied up. Archie ran out from behind the counter, brandishing a baseball bat. There wasn't room in the shop for all the men Macken had brought, they seemed to be using a rotation system, when one fell, two or three more ran in. There was actually an orderly queue of thugs outside – like a nightclub in reverse.

Sara was trying to cover her eyes as Keith swung the carving knife in all directions, using his free hand and his huge head to flatten three other men who ran at him. Macken was standing back watching, a smirk on his face, as Archie and Keith fought off the gang, knowing there were simply too many of them for them to do so indefinitely. One man fell to the floor with blood pouring from a knife wound to the chest, another was slashed viciously across one cheek. I was untying Sara frantically, with Miranda shouting at me to hurry up, Will was getting trampled. Then suddenly I'd freed them both, and Keith and Archie were losing the fight by sheer weight of numbers, and Miranda was on her radio screaming for help and Macken had clocked her.

"Hey!" he yelled. "Get the copper!"

But as he did so, the front door burst open once again and a bearded man burst in, brandishing a revolver. Sara screamed again and Macken backed away, but the man had eyes for only one person in the room. Keith was lying on the floor, held down by four of the gang. The man levelled the gun at Keith's head and fired…

…the gun shot up in his hand and Archie, who was being held upright by three more of the men, crumpled to the floor.

"Archie!" bellowed Keith. "*Archie!*"

Suddenly the gang were in retreat, realising what the gunman's intentions were but not wholly trusting his aim.

"Let's go!" Macken shouted. As they charged past him, the bearded man ran across the room towards Keith, who was trying to get to his feet, but couldn't. Keith fell on to his back, grimacing, his mouth bleeding.

The man stood over him, legs apart, and pointed the gun. Keith looked at him, still grimacing. Then the man fired, six or seven times, emptying the barrel into him with a deafening roar. I covered my eyes and I knew the others had, too.

There was a strange echoing silence, then the sound of police sirens, then Will was suddenly ok and rugby tackling the assassin to the floor outside the shop, then there were more Police UK officers than I'd ever seen in one place and Sara and Miranda and I were hugging one another and crying.

Then I broke free and looked across the room, to where Keith had been shot.

He was lying completely still in those stripy pyjamas and someone had draped a jacket over his face. Archie lay next to him, his eyes staring open, their arms touching as they both lay there dead. There was blood and guts all around them, and my stomach wanted to wretch, but there was something else happening to me.

I was sinking to my knees, sobbing uncontrollably.

And somewhere within that surge of relief and hysteria was a deep, aching sadness for the man who'd taken me on as his apprentice.

65. The funeral

It was at Lawrence's funeral that she saw him again. The 'Frygate' scandal was all over the media and a huge crowd turned out for his second funeral. His wife, Saskia, wasn't one of the crowd, being banged up in prison on charges of insurance fraud. Shirley was in prison too, charged with Lawrence's manslaughter – Rosie wasn't looking forward to being a witness in that case – as a PR officer, she knew how much the media would love the lesbian angle.

Keith's role in the whole thing had become public and she'd seen Sean on the news a couple of times, refusing to be interviewed, looking shy and ordinary again as he tried to ignore reporters' questions. Betsy Saunders had promised to tell the full story in her forthcoming memoirs – after getting out of hospital, she'd stunned colleagues and media alike by announcing her retirement from politics and her engagement to a very dishy doctor from the hospital. And Richard Splash, her old enemy, had been carted off in a police car only this morning in full view of the TV cameras, furiously wrestling with his handcuffs and shrilly protesting his innocence.

They were all there in a little huddle – Sean, Sara, their Mum and Dad, Miranda and her boyfriend, Betsy Saunders herself. Rosie felt like someone on the outside as she stood by the graveside, weeping for poor old Lawrence.

It had been over a week ago that it had all happened. Keith Hartley shot dead in his shop, Sean and Sara having been held captive and nearly killed. Rosie hadn't spoken to any of them about it, she'd read it on the net from France, where she'd gone on a week's impromptu holiday. She hadn't told work either – just sent a couple of postcards. One was addressed to Howard Clarke and said: *Dear Wanker, I quit.* The other was to his PA, Judy. It said: *Glad you're not here. In case your boss didn't get the message, I quit, and he's a wanker. And so are you. Rosie xx*

The funeral was over and Sean was walking away with his family. He looked back slowly, as if to catch one last glimpse of her. You wouldn't think they lived next door to each other.

"Sean!" she called after him.

The whole crew looked around, then looked down at their shoes. Sean waved and hurried over. He bent down awkwardly, as if to hug her, then stopped and took a step back. She held out her hands and he took them. Then she leaned up and kissed him softly on the lips.

"I'm so sorry," he said. "For everything."

"Me too," she said, breaking away again.

He looked confused. "You did nothing wrong."

She smiled as tears threatened. "I did. I was too wrapped up in you sorting out my life to realise you had problems of your own. And I ignored Lawrence's last wish."

"What was that?"

She looked at him evenly, no longer smiling. "To forgive you because you really loved me."

He bowed his head slightly. "You can't always do something just because someone else wants you to."

He looked awkward, tired and sad. She held her hands out again and he took them.

"I just so wish this hadn't happened," she said. "All of it."

He nodded. "I know."

"And I'm so glad you're alive!"

He let his hands slip out of hers. She could see tears at the corners of his eyes.

"So," he said. "What are you doing now?"

"Not much. Jacked in my job! Just been in France for a week, so off to collect Timmy from the cattery. Then home."

He frowned. "France? I thought you'd moved out!"

"No. Just needed some space."

He nodded, still looking sad. "The thing is," he said. "Mum and Dad have offered Sara and me a

place with them in Spain. There's plenty of room
there and you know, this thing has brought us all
closer together…"

"Great. Good for you."

"So I was thinking of saying yes. You know,
fresh start and all that."

She nodded. Sean smiled with real sadness.
Rosie felt a surge emotion welling up as they stood
looking at one another, both unable to break the
gaze.

She put her hand on his arm.

"Stay," she said.

He looked at her softly. "I can't. I couldn't
bear to stay here and not be with you."

And then suddenly she was throwing her
arms around him and crying, and telling him how
much she loved him, how scared she had been that
he was going to die, that she would lose the best
person in her whole life. And he was crying too and
saying he thought he'd blown it, and she was saying
she thought he had too, and then she thought maybe
she had, and they were laughing and crying and
generally making a bit of a scene, but it was a
funeral after all.

He picked her up off the ground and held
her close as she squeezed her arms around his neck
and kissed him. Over his shoulders, she could see

them all smiling – his parents, Sara, Betsy Saunders and her gorgeous fiancé - Christ, even Miranda!

66. The Lawrence Fry Foundation

It's a year now since Keith died. I still think of him sometimes and of the crazy life I led in those days.

Sara moved back to Spain with my parents and the last I heard, she was running a bar over there. Miranda and Will got married a couple of months ago and Rosie and I were there – we still think Will's a smug prick, but Miranda – who for the record again is not fat, but was simply as inept as me at ending a relationship that's best days were behind it – is someone we enjoy seeing. A lot of people we've had contact with, directly or indirectly, are serving jail sentences – Shirley, Richard Splash and Saskia Fry. Splash was convicted of commissioning the attempted murder of Betsy Saunders on my evidence –a sitting MP trying to have another MP bumped off was a double crime and he got five years in a Tesco jail. He also admitted commissioning an unlicensed killer called Niall Burke to shoot Keith – Burke got off with a suspended sentence and a fine. Lee Macken was fined heavily for his attack on Keith's shop and the last I heard, GBH Unlimited had gone into financial meltdown as customers deserted him.

We talk often of Lawrence and the time he spent with us – he's hard to avoid these days as we're both working for the Lawrence Fry Foundation, a campaigning charity set up by Betsy Saunders after she quit politics. It's basically a charity which helps victims of what used to be called crime and their families - and all the publicity that surrounded my own case helped to launch it.

Rosie is Head of PR and I'm Head of Client Care –
and I rarely miss the opportunity to regale audiences
with tales of my own experiences.

I still reflect on the sadness I felt when Keith
was killed. It's something Rosie and Betsy can't
understand – after all, it could have been me, Sara
and Miranda lying dead on his shop floor. But I
don't think I could ever despise Keith as the others
do. He was just a crazy man making a mad living, a
man who didn't care that much about other people –
except me, for some bizarre reason. The more I
think about it, the more I know Keith grew to be
fond of me, though I don't know why. Archie rarely
expanded on anything, but there's part of me that
always wonders what he meant that day, when he
talked about their upbringing and Keith being too
trusting – what made Keith Hartley the man he
was? I'll never know and maybe that's no bad thing.

It's the Foundation's first annual dinner
tonight – Rosie's booked all sorts of celebs and
bands – and the leader of the Opposition, Gregory
Styles, is due to speak. Betsy has told us the man is
a complete prat, but he's the first People's Party
leader to lead the polls since the party was formed.
The only problem is, his policies don't seem that
different from the Government's – like them, he
supports murder, burglary, GBH and almost
anything else you can make money from –
sometimes it seems it's only our Foundation that
doesn't.

As for me and Rosie…there were a few
teething troubles at first. It's not plain sailing
getting things back on track with someone after the

things I did a year ago, but we're going from
strength to strength now. I still wake up some days
and wonder when my luck changed so much that
she's beside me every morning – and that there's
not a cellar full of strangers downstairs who I'm
supposed to have killed. Until life takes another
surreal turn – and who knows what will happen in
the 'New New New Britain' promised by the
People's Party – I just thank my lucky stars that I'm
in a job I can actually do.

Printed in the United Kingdom by
Lightning Source UK Ltd., Milton Keynes
136623UK00001B/181-219/P